Lost Beneath Manhattan

Children's Books by

Sigmund Brouwer

FROM BETHANY HOUSE PUBLISHERS

THE ACCIDENTAL DETECTIVES

The Volcano of Doom
The Disappearing Jewel of Madagascar
Legend of the Gilded Saber
Tyrant of the Badlands
Shroud of the Lion
Creature of the Mists
The Mystery Tribe of Camp Blackeagle
Madness at Moonshiner's Bay
Race for the Park Street Treasure
Terror on Kamikaze Run
Lost Beneath Manhattan
The Missing Map of Pirate's Haven

WATCH OUT FOR JOEL!

Bad Bug Blues
Long Shot
Camp Craziness
Fly Trap
Mystery Pennies
Strunk Soup

www.coolreading.com

04B

Accidental
DETECTIVES
Lost Beneath
Manhattan
SIGMUND BROUWER

BETHANYHOUSE
MINNEAPOLIS, MINNESOTA

Lost Beneath Manhattan

Cover illustration by Chris Ellison
Cover design by Lookout Design Group, Inc.

Published by Bethany House Publishers
11400 Hampshire Avenue South
Bloomington, Minnesota 55438
www.bethanyhouse.com

Bethany House Publishers is a Division of
Baker Book House Company, Grand Rapids, Michigan.

Printed in the United States of America

Lib[illegible] Congress Cataloging-in-Publication Data

[illegible]rouwer, Sigmund, 1959-
Lost beneath Manhattan / by Sigmund Brouwer.
p. cm. — (The Accidental detectives)
Summary: When his younger brother, who had come along on Ricky's class trip to New York City, suddenly disappears, Ricky and his classmates set out to find him.
ISBN 0-7642-2574-X (pbk.)
[1. Lost children—Fiction. 2. New York (N.Y.)—Fiction. 3. Christian life—Fiction. 4. Mystery and detective stories.] I. Title II. Series: Brouwer, Sigmund, 1959- . Accidental detectives.

PZ7.B79984Lo 2004
[Fic]—dc22 2004006165

SIGMUND BROUWER is the award-winning author of scores of books. He speaks to kids around the continent in an effort to instill good reading and writing habits in the next generation. Sigmund and his wife, Cindy Morgan, divide their time between Tennessee and Alberta, Canada.

For Olivia
and the sunshine you bring
into this world

CHAPTER 1

There is something about hearing a rustling in the dark that makes you nervous, even when you are as old as twelve. At first I ignored it. I was lying in my bedroom, about to fall asleep. *No problem, Ricky Kidd,* I told myself, *it's only your imagination.* The noise was probably branches against a window.

So I stared upward in the darkness, wondering about New York City. Actually, dreaming about New York City. Our class had set a goal to go there for a field trip at the end of the school year.

We had washed cars nearly every weekend in September and October and then again in April. We had also done a bottle drive once a month throughout the school year, snow-shoveling marathons, garbage clean-ups, and massive chocolate-bar-selling campaigns. By then I'm sure the entire town of Jamesville wanted our class to go to New York, just so we would leave them alone. Every grown-up in town had a sparkling clean car and a closet full of chocolate bars to replace their long-gone empty bottles.

The only problem was that we were still short. Tomorrow was our last chance to raise the final four hundred dollars we needed. Our teacher, Mr. Evans, had first said if we didn't get enough money, we would cancel the trip and use the funds to paint the school. After we nearly broke his hearing aid by groaning so loud, he said he was only joking. What would really happen was we would go on a field trip to the state capitol instead of to New York City. In other words, it was definitely time to raise another four hundred dollars.

In the dark, though, I didn't lie awake worrying about not getting the money. My friends Mike Andrews and Ralphy Zee had helped me come up with a plan. Lisa Higgins contributed, too, but it's not like we want to give her too much credit—smart girls either drive you nuts or make you blush.

Anyway, at the end of every school year, our school puts on a program to make all the parents happy. I'm not sure it does. Make them happy, that is. I mean, who are we fooling? Singing songs and reciting the answers to mathematical questions isn't exactly great entertainment. I guess it's supposed to prove the teachers are doing their job in teaching, we kids are doing our job in learning, and the parents are doing their job in showing interest.

Instead, my friends and I came up with the Great Theatrical Money-Making Bonanza.

Since the parents were going to be trapped there anyway, we had thought, why not hold a fund-raising play on the same night? Finish the program, put on a play, and then collect donations instead of admission. We hoped if we showed a lot of effort, people would think it was a good cause and *give* more than they would simply pay with an ordinary admission price.

I had spent hours and hours memorizing my lines, so I wasn't worried about actually being in the play. Besides, it was more fun lying in the quiet darkness and dreaming about New York City than worrying.

I'd seen New York plenty of times in movies. It had skyscrapers, subways, movie stars, and professional baseball players. Someone might see Mike and Ralphy and me together, take one look, and decide we were the three to fill the roles of an upcoming Disney movie. For that, I'd even let them put makeup on me and curl my hair.

If not Disney, I'm sure we would settle for doing some

commercials. I could imagine the looks on faces in Jamesville when people saw us on television.

Or maybe I would end up taking a photograph of some awesome news story that would sell to papers all across the world. We could be walking down the street, maybe, and two guys would come running out of a bank with guns in their hands and bags of money over their shoulders. I would snap a couple of photos, capturing the bank robbers' desperation and the terror in the expressions of the bank customers. Then I would calmly toss my camera to a girl standing nearby and briefly catch the adoration on her face before dashing off to track them down. Mike and I would grab skateboards from nearby kids and hook a ride behind the getaway car, holding the bumper and riding the boards and dodging bullets until the car stopped and we tackled the hoods.

There was no telling what could happen. But whatever happened, Mike and Ralphy and I would make the most of it, catching our big break and fearlessly...

When something rustled again, I sat up, not quite daring to believe I had actually heard it. It was nothing, I told myself. Twelve is too old to be worrying about monsters under the bed. How ridiculous.

It came again. A clicking and rustling. *Okay,* I told myself, *you have two options. Put your head under the covers and go to sleep right away. Or carefully make a run for the door.*

The trouble was that the noise came from under my bed. The covers reached all the way to the floor. Even with the lights on, I couldn't see underneath without getting on my knees, lifting the covers, and exposing myself to danger.

Another click and rustle.

I spoke into the darkness. "Boy, oh boy. I can hardly wait to go to the shooting range and practice with my dad again. Last time I was nearly perfect. Maybe tomorrow I'll hit every single target. It's sure nice of Dad to let me sleep with three guns under my pillow."

You can never be too safe with night noises.

There was nothing for a long time. I lay back in bed, but New

York would not get into my head again. The noises must have been a branch, I told myself.

I told myself that eight more times, but it didn't work. So I slipped out of bed without turning on the lights. No sense giving warning, I told myself. I grabbed my baseball bat from the far corner of the room, knelt next to the bed, and gave a couple of little pokes underneath.

Nothing.

What a fool I was. Imagining that branches against the window was maybe a burglar under my bed, waiting for me to fall asleep. Ha, ha, ha.

Ooops.

As I pushed the bat, something pushed back. I think my hair stood straight up. Then the bat was pulled out of my hands.

Nothing like finding a monster under your bed and then arming it.

I stood up and shuffled backward slowly. Fortunately I know where everything is in my room. I can find anything blindfolded. In the darkness, I confidently took another step to grab the doorknob and yank open the door. Instead, I confidently banged my head into the edge of the door. It was like shooting a dozen flashlights into my eyes.

I nearly fell backward into the hallway, then started staggering toward my parents' room for help.

Then something else hit me—the thought that the door had been opened. Whatever was under my bed had come from the hallway. And only one person could do it quietly enough for me not to notice. My six-year-old brother, Joel.

When I snapped on my bedroom lights, pulled the covers off the bed, and looked underneath, Joel blinked at me. His teddy bear, a battered brown with gray-white paws and a white button for the left eye and a black button for the right eye, was beside him. For some reason, it was his only weakness. Some kids gave up teddy bears a lot earlier. Not him. For a while, he'd set it aside for a toy six-shooter and a cowboy outfit, but exciting as that had been for him, he'd been unable to stay away from the ugly little teddy bear.

"Good books," he said, shining my flashlight at the open pages of the library books on New York. My bat was in front of him. "Maybe I can go with you to New York?"

"Don't even think about it." There was no use yelling at Joel about privacy. He can't comprehend the concept. "You cannot go with our class. I repeat. You cannot go with our class. Never. Never. Never. Not in a million years. Understand?"

What a nightmare that would be. Joel in New York City. I rubbed my forehead. Already a bump was rising. "Besides, New York couldn't survive you. Now get back to your room."

I snatched my flashlight from him as he began to walk away.

"And next time, knock."

It was too late. He had already disappeared.

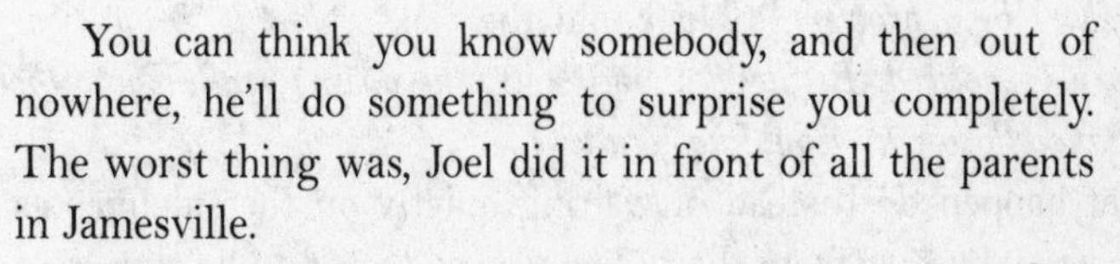

CHAPTER 2

You can think you know somebody, and then out of nowhere, he'll do something to surprise you completely. The worst thing was, Joel did it in front of all the parents in Jamesville.

There our class was, preparing to sing *our* song, when Joel broke in. And all we wanted to do was get the program done quickly so we could start the fund-raising play.

In front of us, in those ugly gray metal chairs that make everybody squirm after two minutes of sitting, were all the parents and relatives. Our small gym was more full than usual for these programs. It made me nervous, but I was happy to see all those donations waiting for us.

Each grade was going to sing one song. Then we older kids were going to have our Great Theatrical Money-Making Bonanza, doing "A Laden Ass and a Horse," which was an Aesop's fable.

It's about a tiny donkey and a horse on a long journey. The donkey is carrying a large load and he begs the horse for some help. The horse refuses. The donkey wears itself out and falls. Then the master takes all of the load off the donkey and puts it on the horse. So instead of sharing the load, the horse has to carry it all by itself.

The moral of the story is that the strong should help the weak. It's fine as morals go, but the real reason we were doing the play was because of the politics. Put on a great play, especially with the moral about helping people—we poor kids, hint, hint—and afterward the donations to our trip would overflow our collection baskets. That was the theory.

Before we could do the play, though, our class needed to wrap up the singing part with "The Star-Spangled Banner." Unfortunately, Joel was nearby. He was the only person we found small enough to fit into the donkey costume with me. Joel was waiting at the side of the stage, ready for his first public appearance in front of a large crowd. He had his teddy bear with him to keep him company. Like I said, most kids give up teddy bears at a lot earlier age.

"It won't be a problem," I had told the class. *"Joel is so quiet, he won't even be noticed. Besides,"* I had said, *"he doesn't really know the words that well, so why would he even try?"*

What happened? Instead of waiting quietly on the sidelines as was expected, he *sang* from there. Joel was so scared to be close to a public appearance that he clutched his teddy bear and sang like his heart was breaking.

The problem was, he got only the first sentence of the song into his head and stayed on those words. When we moved to a nice melodious "By the dawn's early light," he stayed on "Oh, say, can you see." Just like a stuck record. And since he was scared, he was loud.

The strange part for the people watching was that they couldn't see Joel, and they didn't know where our singing competition was coming from.

We moved on to "What so proudly we hailed," and still he stayed on "Oh, say, can you see." And got louder about it. He nearly drowned out our "By the twilight's last gleaming."

All the kids glared at me, and those next to me poked my ribs, but there was nothing I could do. Our only choice was to get louder ourselves. Instead of singing, it became a yelling contest.

There were friendly faces out there, as if they really liked our singing anyway. There were Mom and Dad, of course, and my baby sister, Rachel. But their smiles didn't count, because family always has to pretend they are enjoying themselves at events like these. But even old Mr. Frederick, the town grump, had a smile on his face. Mr. Frederick is a retired banker, and he hates kids, dogs, ice cream, laughter, and anything else fun. He spends most of his time sitting on his porch and guarding his lawn against anyone brave enough to try a shortcut across it. I think he comes to the school programs so that he can put kids' names with faces—if someone gets away with a crab apple or two, he knows whose parents to call.

Finally the last of Joel's "Oh, say, can you see," which he had sung for what seemed like five minutes straight, stopped echoing across the school gym. The curtain went down so we could prepare for the play. I took another couple of pokes in the ribs for Joel's performance, and then we all scrambled into action.

Joel was still white-faced from singing scared, so I let him keep his teddy bear as we suited ourselves into the donkey costume.

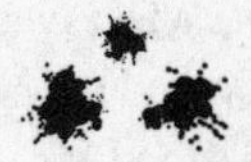

"Please, good sir, I beg of thee to help carry my burdens; otherwise forsooth I fear I shall die," I said. I waited for Mike, who was the front end of the horse, to reply. Ralphy was the back end of their horse costume.

"Beg all thoust wants, lowly donkey. My station in life is not one of a beast of burden."

It's not easy seeing through donkey eyes. Still, as I looked across the gym, I could see my dad. He was imitating our lines to Mom. Not that I blamed him. He'd been listening to me practice in front of the mirror for hours. Mom elbowed him.

"But, good sir, thou art so mighty," I said in my best protesting voice. Acting isn't easy. "And I am so weak. For thee to ease my burden would take so little of thine strength. And it would mean so much to the likes of me."

Even though a person likes the chance to be a star, I didn't know if it was better to be a talking donkey or a background tree. Trees didn't have many lines to memorize. Trees could also stand in one spot and not worry about their costume.

Donkeys and horses, on the other hand, had major concerns. First of all, Old English. *Forsooth*s and *thou*s until you wanted to scream. Why not: *Hey, dude, lighten my load before I croak*?

The bigger concern was the costumes. They were designed for both kids inside to be standing up. That way, a tall kid at the front was high enough to be the neck and head. A short kid at the back only needed to be tail high. But try walking in coordination, especially with a load between you, and very especially when the back end of you would rather carry a teddy bear than a stack of wooden boxes designed to look like a killing burden. Which they were.

"Forsooth, thou impertinent beast," Mike sneered. "Bother me no more lest I deliver thou a kick so mightily that the cops stop you for speeding thirty miles away."

Thanks, Mike, good control of Old English there. Lisa Higgins, who was acting as the master, stomped on Mike's foot.

"Please, for the last time, good sir, I beseech—" Something had bumped the top of my leg and rolled down to my ankle. The icy cold that gripped me in panic also froze my tongue. *Don't be what I think it is*, I told myself.

This time, Lisa stomped *my* foot.

"Say what?" Mike the horse asked, prompting me for my line.

Great. It *was* the teddy bear. We were in big trouble.

That teddy bear is Joel's only weakness. When he's asleep, you can have a band playing in his room or wave a good-smelling hot dog under his nose, and he won't wake up. Wriggle one paw of his teddy bear and he sits up instantly, staring at you with big accusing eyes.

When I'm mad at Joel, I remind him that teddy bear stuffing is hard to replace. It gets his attention. But I could never hurt the bear because I remember Joel's face the day Old Man Jacobsen's dog snuck away with it. Joel began digging in all the dog's favorite hiding spots with his plastic toy garden shovel. He wouldn't let me help. Even the dog was smart enough to stay out of sight. Joel's face was muddy with tears and dirt by the time he found the teddy bear. Then he gave it to me to wash, and we were both happy.

The good thing is, Joel thinks if the teddy bear can't see, nobody can see the teddy bear. When he wants to hide it, he covers the bear's eyes, so it's easy to kidnap. When I need to be alone, I put the teddy bear into the dryer. Joel sits and watches it tumble until the cycle ends.

In other words, Joel without his teddy bear is a desperate person, and I knew that too well as I felt something furry against my leg.

I whispered into the costume, "Wait, Joel. I'll get it for you."

Mike the horse got confused. He nodded to the audience and said loudly, "You were about to beseech?"

I felt movement behind me.

"Joel, wait!" I hissed. It was too late. He was already squirming ahead.

Mike repeated himself. "Donkey, I said, *you were about to beseech!*"

There were three seconds of silence. This was the part where I was supposed to groan and waver with weariness. Then Lisa would transfer the load onto the horse.

Our timing was bad. Lisa decided it was time to take the load off me even though I hadn't gone into a dramatic waver.

Halfway through the transfer, Joel couldn't wait and he made his move. So I tried to reach into my donkey leg to help him.

Joel nearly crawled into my leg while I was turning around. That's the trouble with younger brothers. You can never depend on them.

We bumped heads. Mine was still tender from where I had walked into the door the night before.

I moaned.

Joel scrambled forward into my donkey leg.

I was holding my head as I started to fall. I let go of my head and grabbed for balance at Mike the horse. He grabbed at Lisa to keep from falling with me. That scared Ralphy into jumping half out of the costume into two trees, who fell forward trying to get away—

and they knocked two other trees right back into Mike and Lisa and me.

When it finally ended, only Lisa was standing. And she let the load of wooden boxes fall on Mike and me.

"Woe is me!" Mike cried from where he was buried under the broken boxes. It was the only part he had left to say. "What suffering I have brought upon myself. I would not share a lighter load, and look what has become of me."

Joel ignored Mike and fished around in my donkey leg until he came up with the teddy bear. Then he wriggled out of the donkey suit and walked off the stage without looking back.

Mom said later she thought Mr. Frederick was going to crack his face after not laughing so hard in decades. Not that people were noticing right then, because they were all hysterical by that time anyway.

Which didn't bode well for our money-making part of the Bonanza.

CHAPTER 3

"Ralphy, you *have* to go out there."

It was collection time a few minutes later. I'm not sure why we were even going to try. Joel's presence had ended in its usual disaster.

As a brother, I have to admit Joel's okay. I mean, he even wears white high-top sneakers, blue jeans, and T-shirts because he wants to copy me. But Joel's worse than a tiny ghost. Ralphy and Mike are twelve like me, and we still know better than to relax when he's around.

Joel never says much when you do manage to spot him. He just stares and watches. It seems he can get through locked doors and closed windows. He disappears as soon as you turn your head and then appears again when you least expect it. Which is usually when you're doing something you shouldn't. Those are the times I faint or have heart attacks. Or fall into disaster.

Joel's latest effort had turned Ralphy into a thin white bundle of shaking nerves.

"But all those people," Ralphy protested. "After that mess, how can we face them with a basket asking for money?"

"We have no choice," I said. "Otherwise, no New York. Not that we have much chance now anyway."

Poor Ralphy. Mike and I often forget how Ralphy, so

good on computers, tends to get nervous about anything else. He is skinny, with straight hair that points in every direction except for where it's supposed to. The back of his shirt always hangs out, and he gets yelled at for it by his older sisters, who spend so much time painting their fingernails and worrying about what dress to wear that I'm surprised they can find the time to yell at him. They yell at him a lot, and they sneak up behind him every time they have something to yell about, so we understand why he's the nervous type.

Worse, his nervousness makes everything more difficult for him. He's the one who will get stuck halfway up a tree, or get his shirt caught on the Bradleys' fence just as their German shepherds come rushing up to bark at us.

He sighed, took his basket, and left the stage to face his public.

My job was worse. I had to go back on the stage and begin cleaning up.

People were still laughing.

I kept my face down as I picked up the broken props. Mike and Ralphy and a few others in our class were moving up and down the aisles.

Would we get the four hundred dollars we needed? I didn't have much hope about that. Which made cleaning up even more lousy.

The only consolation was that Lisa was helping me. Usually, she's as much trouble as Joel, but at least I wasn't alone in front of all those people.

The problem, first of all, is that she's pretty. So you never know whether to like her as a friend, or what. Lisa has long dark hair, which she ties in a ponytail to play baseball. When she smiles, it's sunshine breaking through clouds. Her smile is so nice to see, there are times—when she hasn't made me look stupid for a while—that

I look for ways to put that smile on her face. Not that I would ever admit it to Mike or Ralphy.

The second problem is that she is good at sports. Of course, we can't let her know it. Mike says it's luck whenever she hits a home run, but I know better. Lisa's the type of person who watches baseball on television to learn from the best, and then she practices what she sees on her own until she's confident enough to use it against us. Unfortunately, it works.

Which leads to the biggest trouble of all. If Lisa's on the other team, it's almost guaranteed you will lose—not that anyone will admit that, either. But how can you publicly fight over getting a girl on your team? Especially if she's pretty and once in a while you catch yourself staring at her because of it.

The answer is that you can't. So you negotiate hard to get her on your team, while pretending hard that you don't want her, and it wastes a half hour of playing time.

And last of all, every time I do something stupid, she finds out. Like losing a teddy bear in a donkey costume and wrecking an entire fund-raising play.

She must have been able to read my face.

"Don't worry, Ricky. It's not *all* your fault."

"Wonderful," I said.

Then she grinned to show she was teasing. "It will work out somehow," she said.

It turned out she was right. But I'm not sure that made me happy, either.

Ralphy and Mike came running up as we were nearly finished cleaning. Most of the people had left by then, and the money was counted.

"Good news and bad news," Mike announced.

"Wonderful," I said.

"Bad news first," Lisa said.

Mike said, "We collected much more money than anyone expected, especially with what happened."

"That's bad news?"

"It was only two hundred and seventy-five dollars."

That *was* bad news.

"However," Mike continued, "the good news is that we're still going to New York City."

I should have been suspicious right then.

"Great!" I said. It was enough that somehow we would make it there. All my dreaming wouldn't be wasted.

Lisa, of course, couldn't leave well enough alone.

"What's the catch, Mike?"

He grinned his fox grin. *And* Ralphy was smirking. Even with that, I didn't recognize approaching trouble.

"Mr. Evans and I were standing there, wondering how to come up with the extra money, when Mr. Frederick stopped by."

I frowned. Ralphy's smirk widened.

"Mr. Frederick?"

Mike nodded. "Yup. He asked us if we needed any money and if we did, could he donate the rest."

"But he's a scrooge and hates kids."

Lisa nodded agreement with me.

"Maybe, but he wrote a check for the difference and told us to have fun."

"I can't believe it," I said.

"Neither can I," Lisa repeated.

"There must be a catch," I said.

"Yup." Mike snorted. "There was a condition, all right. Mr. Frederick said he was donating the money because he can't remember the last time he enjoyed an evening out as much as this one. He said that what did it was the Aesop's fable."

"The play? But we wrecked it."

Ralphy tightened his lips to hold back his grin. "Mr. Frederick didn't think so. He said they've been running school programs for twenty years and he hates them. He said he had never laughed so hard, and it was thanks to one person. He said if that one person could go to New York with our class as a reward, the money was ours."

My blood turned to ice.

"Mr. Evans thought it was fine," Ralphy continued. "Mr. Evans said he couldn't see a problem taking someone as quiet and well-behaved as Joel."

I groaned.

No, not Joel. . . .

CHAPTER 4

There's not much glamour to watching the New York Yankees play the Toronto Blue Jays when you're sitting in the stands holding a teddy bear.

Everything else was great, though. The sun was beaming down on us in the bleachers. There was the noisy buzz of fans yelling at players. A slight breeze made the big flag in the corner of the field wave majestically, and it cooled our faces nicely. The smell of popcorn and hot dogs filled our noses. And the game was close and exciting. Who could ask for more?

Nobody. Except Mike.

"Hey, Ricky. It's your turn to get another couple hot dogs."

Craaaack! I missed seeing the hit because Mike had poked me in the ribs. Toronto scored a run.

Mike is a dangerous friend to have. He thinks the word *impossible* applies to anything that grown-ups don't want kids to try. Like juggling chain saws. Any grown-up will tell you it's impossible to juggle chain saws. Which, of course, it is.

If you told Mike it's impossible to juggle chain saws, he'd look through all the garages in our town of Jamesville to borrow enough to begin his act, then find a place to charge admission, and somehow make it look like my idea.

He's a little bigger than I am. And he's got this rule about sneakers—they can't match. His left shoe is always a different color than his right shoe, and he has more pairs to choose from than I have comic books. At least it seems that way. I just wish sometimes the shoes would match the colors of his Hawaiian shirts. When he whizzes by on a skateboard, it hurts my eyes to watch him. Mike also has a crazy grin and dusty red hair, so after seeing him, nothing he does ever surprises people. It makes them mad once in a while, but it never surprises them.

"Let me watch the game, Mike. Wait for the hot dog guy to come by."

"So he can throw another one in my lap and bug us about our baseball gloves? No, thanks."

It probably did look funny. All twenty-three of us wore baseball gloves in one hand and ate popcorn with the other. Even Mr. Evans had one. You never knew when a foul ball could shoot into the stands. Sure, we probably looked stupid, and yes, baseball gloves take a lot of room in your suitcase. But you only get to see a game like this once.

Even Joel was on the edge of his seat. And it takes a declared emergency to get him to lift an eyebrow.

Being at the game was so exciting, we weren't tired. We should have been. It was Wednesday afternoon. To get to the ball game, we had left Jamesville by bus for the airport at five o'clock that morning, flown to LaGuardia Airport, which is between Queens and the Bronx part of New York City, and taken a commuter train to our hotel on Long Island. After checking in, we had taken the train back through Long Island, and from there we had taken the subway and a public bus to the ballpark.

Everything was exciting, in fact. It was the first time in an airplane for most of us. Ralphy trotted to the bathroom at the back of the plane a million times. Joel and his stupid teddy bear got cuddled by good-looking flight attendants. Whenever I pointed out that I was his brother, they said, *"That's nice,"* ignored me, and cuddled him some more. *I* knew he wasn't as scared as he acted.

Flying over the city had riveted us to the airplane windows. When the plane banked for a turn, the skyscrapers against the blue sky seemed ready to scratch the belly of our plane.

As we rode the public transportation in New York, Mr. Evans said he had a hard time deciphering graffiti, so he didn't explain any of the words to us. The other chaperones, Mrs. Thompson and Mrs. Bradley, were too busy smiling nervously at all the mean and scruffy-looking people, so they didn't discuss graffiti with us, either.

Hotels near the center of New York are real expensive. I heard breakfast alone there costs as much as I make in one week of delivering papers. To afford this trip, our class had to stay at a hotel on Long Island thirty miles from downtown Manhattan. That killed me. *Thirty miles.* And every inch of it was covered with cars and trucks and buildings and people. By the time we reached the hotel, my mouth was dry from hanging open in amazement so long.

It meant we had to spend an hour going into Manhattan and an hour getting out each day. We had Thursday, Friday, and half of Saturday before our plane left again. That shows how much it costs to travel. Ten months of hard work traded for four days of sightseeing. Well worth it, we thought, especially sitting in the bright sunshine watching the New York Yankees.

I was especially waiting for my hero, Dan Stubbing, to hit a home run. Once he had been at a sportsmen's dinner in Jamesville, and he was really nice. After the dinner, he took a few minutes to sign my baseball bat and show me the correct way to swing. I had fifteen of his baseball cards, and I watched for him on television all the time and cheered for him.

Right now, though, I was sad for him. He was in a terrible slump. He had had only six hits in the last twenty games and only one home run in the last thirty games. The newspapers said he should retire.

"I'll pay for the hot dogs if you get them," Mike said.

Not a bad deal.

"Okay, Mike, but don't let Joel have his teddy bear. It's our only way of keeping him around."

One, I wasn't going for hot dogs carrying a teddy bear. Two, if Joel went wandering now, it would be the biggest nightmare in the world.

When I got back, my hands filled with ketchup-leaking, mustard-dripping hot dogs, Joel was gone. That didn't bother me. Everybody else was gone, too.

I could see them scrambling three rows up, where the bleachers were empty. Naturally, someone hit a foul ball into the stands when I was getting the hot dogs.

It took them a few minutes to settle down. Ralphy was holding the baseball. It had hit someone's glove and bounced off Ralphy's head. He didn't know whether to grin from happiness or grimace from pain.

Mike grabbed a hot dog and stuffed half into his mouth.

My legs turned weak with a sudden thought.

"Mike, where's the teddy bear?"

"Ummm-uggh-lummm."

"Mike, where's Joel?"

His eyes widened. He swallowed in a big gulp.

"I put the teddy bear down for just a second. Honest. We all started running for the ball and I forgot about Joel."

Mike knew as well as I did what this meant. Joel disappears any-time he wants in a place as small as Jamesville. He would be impos-sible to find here among thousands and thousands of yelling and cheering strangers. And would the strangers be as nice to him as everyone in Jamesville?

We looked in all directions. Joel really was gone. I felt sick. Sud-denly it didn't matter to me that Dan Stubbing would be the third batter up in the next inning.

Mike stood beside Ralphy and said, "I'll tell Mr. Evans. It's my fault. I'll take the blame. Mr. Evans will be mad at having to miss part of the game, but he'll know what to do. Joel will be back right away. I promise."

I grabbed his arm and thought for a second. Joel wouldn't leave the stadium. If Mr. Evans had to go to the authorities, it didn't make any difference if he did it now or two innings from now. We might as well let Mr. Evans and the rest of the class enjoy as much of the game as possible.

I explained it that way to Mike. He nodded slowly.

"There are four innings left in the game," I said. "You, me, and Ralphy will split up and look for him. In two innings we'll meet back here. If we don't have Joel by then, we ask for help."

Mike and Ralphy nodded.

A quiet and soft voice from behind spoke into my ear. "I'll help, too."

With the whisper, there was the soft smell of perfume and the light touch of hair against my neck. I nearly turned around and hugged Lisa for being so nice.

We left in four directions. For a while, I had thought the most important thing was watching Dan Stubbing at bat so I could cheer and shout for my hero. It just goes to show how sometimes you forget what really matters.

I wanted my brother back.

CHAPTER 5

Think, I told myself. I had already been looking for over an inning. If I couldn't find Joel in the next fifteen minutes . . .

Think. Come on, think. Then I shook my head and sighed. *Boy, oh boy, Ricky Kidd, when you get wrapped up, you really get wrapped up in yourself. Pray first, then think.*

Not that I think praying to God solves your problems instantly. Like, if you're falling off a cliff, praying is going to get you a parachute?

But there are times to pray, and when you think about it, it's incredible.

Would you casually walk up to the president of the United States to tell him you're feeling bad and would like help getting through a rough spot? Not likely, I'll bet. First of all, you wouldn't get the time to talk to someone that important. He has secretaries for his secretaries. Then, just seeing that big limousine and the beautiful mansion and going through the wide, quiet hallways would be enough to make you tremble at how important the president is.

And here's God, who is not only in charge of the country, but the world and the billions of stars in the universe, and not only that, but He was the One who made it all in the first place. And we can talk to Him anytime, starting off with *Dear Lord.* When you think about it, it takes your breath away.

So I wasn't going to ask, *Please, God, make Joel appear in front of my eyes this instant.* I just prayed, *Lord, I'm pretty scared for my brother, and could you please watch over him while all of us try to find him?* I mean, we people have to do our part, too.

"Hey, kid, watch where you're going, you lousy creep!"

I had just stepped on a fat man's foot. He didn't seem like he was in the mood to hear why I had my eyes closed. I smiled politely and started scanning again for Joel.

The bobbing as people sat and stood and walked and cheered was like looking across a huge cornfield blowing in the wind. How could anyone spot a six-year-old kid in that crowd?

Then it occurred to me that the answer was, you didn't. Instead, you put yourself in Joel's place.

I tried to ignore the excitement inside me as I realized something. What would be logical for Joel to do? He was more curious than a dozen cats, and here was everybody looking down and watching one thing. The baseball game. Wouldn't Joel want to do the same thing, except at much closer range?

I headed down the aisle.

When I reached the bottom of the stands, right down at field level, a guard stopped me.

"You got a ticket for this section, kid?" He had a big belly, a shirt with sweat circles spreading in all directions, and a mean snarl.

"No, I'm sorry. I've got a lost brother."

"Then beat it. I hear that excuse all the time. You kids will do anything to get near the players."

"But it's not an excuse!"

"Beat it, kid."

"He's about this tall"—I said desperately, placing my hand chest high—"and carries a brown-and-white teddy bear."

Suddenly the guard grabbed my arm! Before I could shout or even faint, he had dragged me down three more steps!

He stopped in front of another guard. I was still too shocked to say anything.

"Take this kid," the big-bellied man said to the second guard. "He goes with the one that had a teddy bear."

At least they knew where Joel was. That made me feel better. A bit better. What kind of trouble had he landed in?

"You're in for it now," the second guard said. He took my arm and led me under the stands.

We walked through a narrow dark hallway. It turned a couple ways, and I lost all sense of direction. What had Joel done? Did baseball stadiums have torture chambers? Every time I tried asking a question, the guard said, "You'll have to wait."

We came to a door. The guard unlocked it, opened it, thrust me through, and followed me. The sunlight that pounded my eyes made me stagger.

We were . . . in the . . . players' dugout?

"Who's this, Fred?" The man was old and bald and had on a Yankee baseball uniform. He spat on the ground after asking the question.

"The kid's looking for his brother. I thought maybe Dan could help him out."

We really were in the Yankees' dugout! I nearly fainted.

It seemed like I was in a forest of huge men, all wearing Yankee baseball uniforms. There were baseball bats and white-on-black team jackets scattered over the benches.

Most of the men ignored me. They were all facing the field, watching the game.

"Sure, send him down."

The guard pointed to the end of the players' dugout. "You'll find him there."

I trembled as I walked past the players. A few nodded in my direction. I had to step carefully to miss big wads of tobacco spit.

There, standing near the top of the steps that led to the field, was Joel. Another baseball player was standing with him, gently holding him back by the shoulders.

"Uh, hi," I said. Why was Joel anxious to get on the field? He's usually as shy as a deer.

"This your brother, kid?"

I nodded. It still seemed like a dream. How did Joel end up in the players' dugout of the New York Yankees, and was I really standing here talking to one of the players?

"Hold him, will ya? Stubbing's up to bat next, and if he gets a hit, I'm out there next to warm up."

The player shook his head. "What am I saying? The tying run's on second and the go-ahead run's at first and Stubbing's in the hitter's circle. I don't need to worry about going out there. Stubbing won't get a hit to save us. He's washed up."

I moved to the top of the steps anyway. From there I could see two things. I could see why the crowd was roaring and clapping with laughter. And I could see why Joel wanted to scoot onto the field.

Dan Stubbing, my hero, was carrying his bat as he approached the plate. He was also carrying Joel's teddy bear.

How many times can a guy come close to fainting in one afternoon, anyway?

"I don't get it." My voice squeaked. Joel frowned at me for breaking his concentration. He had eyes only for his teddy bear.

"Neither do I," the player said. "Stubbing sees this kid in the stands, hollers for a guard to bring him down, spends a few minutes talking even though the kid doesn't say a word, then Stubbing takes the dumb bear out there with him.

"Yankee Stadium, and he takes a teddy bear to bat. When a guy falls apart, he falls apart completely."

Great. My hero is up to bat and he takes my brother's teddy bear. Not exactly what dreams are made of. I almost forgot where I was—until the roar of the crowd deepened to a thunder that sent chills down my spine. Dan Stubbing had just hit a home run!

So this is what it sounds like to a baseball player. What a thrill.

The ball flew in a high, graceful arc against the blue of the sky and disappeared in the far stands.

All of us in the dugout jumped up and down and cheered with

the crowd. The two players on base crossed home plate. The Yankees had pulled ahead!

We forgot about Joel. The jumping and cheering made it easy for his escape. He beelined for his teddy bear.

Old people say they have special memories. They can close their eyes and bring the memory back as if it just happened. I'm not sure I like that. Between Dan Stubbing circling the bases and Joel's calm trot to the teddy bear, it was embarrassing from where I stood. Do I want to be in a rocking chair someday and have to see *that* all over again whenever I think about New York?

Joel dusted off his teddy bear at home plate and scowled at Dan Stubbing, and the umpire took off his face mask in disbelief.

Dan took Joel by the hand and led him back to the dugout.

"This your brother?" he asked me.

I nodded.

"I don't suppose he'll sell me the teddy bear, huh?"

I shook my head, too stunned to speak. Was all this really happening?

Dan Stubbing sighed. "Any chance we can at least get him to talk?"

CHAPTER 6

"Mike, I'm sorry. I'm sorry I didn't ask Dan Stubbing to invite our whole class into the clubhouse. I'm sorry I didn't get all the players to pose for a photograph with us. And I'm especially sorry I forgot to tell Dan Stubbing your batting average is .856. Okay? I'm sorry."

"Sorry's not enough," Mike said. "I can't believe you were right there and you didn't think about your friends. Especially if my batting average might get him to send a scout to Jamesville."

"Right!" Ralphy giggled. "But then you'd have to tell him that the average doesn't include all your at-bats when Lisa struck you out."

"Girls don't count," Lisa said before Mike could use his only defense.

"Hmmmph." Mike scowled at all of us. I didn't worry. All I had to do was tell him the Dan Stubbing story for the hundredth time, and he would forget about being mad.

We were riding the commuter train from Long Island into Manhattan. It was Thursday morning, and our next sight-seeing point was the Statue of Liberty. In the afternoon we were going to the Empire State Building and then the Museum of Modern Art.

Would I have changed things if I could have known what was about to happen along the way? Of course, but that's as silly as wishing you could go back in time and start things over.

I was quickly learning to think of New York City in terms of boroughs. There are five: Manhattan, a long narrow island that is the center of the city; Bronx, north and east of Manhattan; Queens, across the East River from Manhattan; Brooklyn, south of Queens; and Staten Island, sometimes called Richmond.

Before this trip I had thought towns ended when the buildings ended, like Jamesville—the houses quit at the edge of a field and the next town starts about ten miles down the road. In New York City, cross a street and you're in another city. And the cities go on, one after the other, forever.

West, across the Hudson River from Manhattan, was New Jersey, with dozens of cities fanning in all directions. On the New York side, the Long Island cities—one after the other—stretched east of Manhattan as the island extended into the Atlantic Ocean. North of Manhattan and the Bronx, city after city stretched in yet another direction. Millions and millions of people. I wondered how God kept track of them all.

I was surprised at how dirty and gray the old buildings seemed as the train clacked and shook along the tracks through Queens on our approach to Manhattan. The day before, the same trip had been so exciting that everything seemed polished and glamorous. Funny, too, that I was just noticing the stale, sweaty smell and the littered papers inside the commuter train.

Mike interrupted my thoughts.

"So maybe you didn't remember to give Dan Stubbing my batting average. Can I at least keep the autographed baseball at my house for a while?"

Ralphy broke in. "Do you really believe his story about the home run?"

"Yup." I had a feeling I was going to be able to tell this story in my sleep. "When you think about it, it makes sense."

Ralphy, Mike, and Lisa leaned in to listen.

"Dan Stubbing told me that when he was our age, he was in a

Little League championship game. At the time, it was the most important game of his life, and he was so nervous about it, he didn't sleep for two nights before, and he threw up three times the day of the game.

"Then his mom did something really strange. For days she had tried telling him that no game in the world was worth getting that upset. It wasn't working, so finally she brought something down from the attic. It was a teddy bear. She told him that Dan had once thought the beat-up little teddy bear was the most important thing in the world. She told him that his love for the bear was a lot more worthwhile than worrying about a baseball game. She said people grow old and games become less important, but that love is something you never lose."

I took a breath. By the way Mike and Ralphy and Lisa were ignoring the buildings and bridges flashing past our window, I knew they weren't tired of the story, even though I had told it ten times the night before.

"Dan Stubbing's teddy bear, huh?"

I nodded at Mike.

"Yeah. She was so mad at Dan for caring that much about a baseball game that she took the teddy bear into the stands with her when she went to watch. She waved it at Dan as he went to bat with the bases loaded. He didn't get mad or embarrassed. He suddenly realized she was right."

Mike broke in. "And instead of wanting a home run so bad that he tried too hard and choked, he relaxed."

"Exactly," I said. "And we know how that works. When you're relaxed, you swing easy. When you swing easy, presto. Hit after hit. He hit a grand slam home run as she waved that teddy bear all those years ago."

"And when Dan saw Joel in the stands with his teddy . . ." Lisa let her voice fade as she replayed Dan Stubbing's home run in her mind.

". . . he remembered the lesson his mom had taught him when he was twelve. Suddenly it didn't matter so much that he was in a slump. There were more important things to worry about than hitting home runs.

"It made him feel so good to remember, he got a guard to take Joel into the dugout. Then he borrowed Joel's teddy bear and—"

"Hit the next pitch right out of the ball park!" Ralphy always got excited at this part of the story.

"That's right." I sat back and relaxed. Dan had gotten the entire team to autograph a baseball for me. I promised to time-share it with Ralphy and Mike and Lisa. Dan had given an autographed bat to Joel.

It was an ending to the nightmare of Joel's disappearance that I could still hardly believe. A nice ending. But it made me determined to watch Joel even closer for the rest of the trip.

The clacking and shaking slowed. Our train hit darkness. Penn Station, where dozens of different train tracks met and ended underneath the streets. We were about to take the subway to the ferry that ran out to Liberty Island.

It shouldn't be hard to keep track of a six-year-old kid with a teddy bear, right? Five minutes later Joel was gone again.

I wasn't sure I could ever forgive Mr. Frederick for sending him on this trip with us.

CHAPTER 7

Joel being gone didn't give me much time to think about distracting Ralphy.

Mike and I had found a little joke shop near our hotel. It sold great gags, and we found a fake camera on sale. It looked like a real camera, but when you hit the shutter, it squirted water. It was battery operated so that the water would shoot at least twenty feet.

Ralphy loved clicking pictures of people with his real camera. It didn't matter if he knew them or not. He liked catching the expressions on their faces when they weren't looking. Which meant sometimes we looked goofy in shots when he caught us sleeping or sneezing or something.

The trick camera, we figured, would get him back for all the times he made us look stupid in photographs. Once, just once, he'd squirt someone and get in trouble. Then Mike and I would take the camera back and use it ourselves on unsuspecting people. After all, why waste a good investment?

We weren't worried that Ralphy would notice the difference once we made the switch. Ralphy sometimes forgets to see the forest because he worries about the trees. I guess computer people can be like that. He'd concentrate on the photo and not the camera. All we needed to do was distract him, get in his knapsack when he wasn't looking, and trade cameras.

With Joel gone, though, I had better things to worry about. Worse, I had let him hold his teddy bear during the train ride. Now I didn't even have a hostage to bring him back. *How can a kid melt away like that?*

We were in the huge open area in the middle of the station. It was dim because we were underground and the fluorescent lights were dirty. It was noisy, too, with trains coming and going and with instructions coming over the loudspeakers.

As a group, we were slowly moving toward the escalators that led to the subway tracks. It was the kind of place that no matter how crowded it is—which it was—you still feel lonely. That was a strange feeling for me.

Where is Joel? If I didn't spot him in ten seconds, I'd stop Mr. Evans. That would hold up the whole class, but I had no choice.

There! Out of the corner of my eye, I caught movement. By the water fountain!

"Mike," I hissed. "Make sure you guys don't take off without me. I've got to get Joel."

"But I thought he was right behind us."

"Dream on," I said. "I think I'm going to buy a leash for him." Later, I wished I had. "Just get everyone to wait, okay? This shouldn't take long, but you never know with Joel."

He nodded. "Don't forget about Ralphy's camera."

I winked. "No problem. I'll be right back."

I turned to corral Joel, but already he was disappearing into a small hallway our class had just passed. I forced a sigh through gritted teeth.

Something made me slow down as I approached the corner. Maybe it was remembering how creepy the hallway had looked when we went by. It was dark and the floor was littered with paper. My guess was that it led to the back entrances of the doughnut shops and gift stores in the station.

I stuck my head around the corner to look. When my eyes adjusted, I could see Joel bent over and pulling at something.

I stepped closer, and Joel looked up from his position down the hallway and frowned.

"Hard work, Ricky. You help?"

He was tugging at two feet on the ground that were sticking out of a doorway!

I broke into a short run.

"Joel. No!"

It would have been too late, except the person who owned the feet didn't move.

The person who owned the feet smelled, too. Smelled awful.

But Joel was tugging at his feet and almost crying, he was so worried about the fallen grown-up. Even though the kid was driving me nuts, a wave of affection hit me. How could you not like someone so determined to go through life fixing broken wings and feeding stray animals?

When I saw the man, I understood why Joel looked worried. Was the man sick or dying? His clothes were a filthy brown, and his face was pinched and white, even with the short, dirty beard on his cheeks.

The man looked no different than the shapeless people we had seen on the streets begging for money or digging through garbage. Some of the beggars even had small children with them. Manhattan was pretty, but it was sure opening my eyes with some of its sad things.

Joel was so concerned, he had placed his teddy bear on the man's chest. Just like he did whenever I was sick and at home in bed. Beside the man was a coffee cup filled with water, Joel's reason for being at the fountain.

"Stand back, Joel. And wait here. I'll get help."

I made the short dash back to the main area and stopped a man in a business suit.

I pointed into the hallway. "Excuse me, sir, someone's in trouble back there."

The man ignored me and kept walking.

To a lady in high heels and a nice dress: "Ma'am, could you take a look? I think someone back there needs help."

She smiled politely and stepped around me.

In the next minute crowds of people walked past the entrance to the dark hallway, and not one person stopped. *What to do? What if the man is dying? Doesn't anyone care?*

What made me give up was noticing that Joel had moved into the doorway with the man.

I walked back.

Before I got close enough, I heard Joel. "Have water, okay? Make you good again."

There was a splashing.

The feet moved and I heard a groan.

More splashing.

"What the—! Hey, kid, beat it!"

Joel giggled. "Good! You're not dead!"

Then a sickly roar. "What's this?!"

Joel's bear flashed by my face as the man lying in the doorway snarled and flung it across the hallway.

Joel nearly tripped over my feet following it. He picked up the teddy bear and looked back at the man with a perplexed smile.

Unlike Jamesville, around here people actually slept in places other than a bed. And nobody seemed to care. Why would God actually let things like this happen?

I didn't have time to wonder. There was another roar.

Anybody strong enough to yell and throw a teddy bear wasn't dying, I told myself. In fact, anybody who sounded that angry probably wasn't in the mood to be rescued.

The feet disappeared from the hallway as the man pulled himself up.

"He's a little grumpy," I said to Joel, grabbing his hand. "Maybe it's time to run."

We did.

CHAPTER 8

If a person could ever know ahead of time when a disaster was about to hit . . .

Already it was Thursday afternoon, halfway through our tour of the Museum of Modern Art, and it seemed as if we had just arrived in the city.

We had seen the Statue of Liberty and the Empire State Building, and we had walked through Manhattan for hours before getting to the Museum of Modern Art, but not once had we bumped into any Walt Disney movie directors wanting to give us roles. And we hadn't interrupted any bank robberies, either.

I was beginning to wonder why I had even kept my camera ready for action during our walk. Sure, there were the shiny limousines, but I had already used a roll of film on them. Besides, the drivers weren't nice about getting out and posing beside their cars.

The skyscrapers I had dreamed of were there, too, but after looking through my camera once, I had given up on them. They absolutely filled the viewfinder. All you could see was wall. Not much point in shooting that.

At street level, I could have taken dozens and dozens of pictures of people. People in fur coats and limousines. People in rags and digging through garbage. But it didn't feel right interfering with their privacy, so mostly I watched. It made me feel terrible to see people sitting on corners and pleading for nickels and dimes.

In fact, most of my other photos had been of Lisa. Her at the Statue of Liberty. Her alongside the commuter train. Her at the hotel pool. All by accident, of course.

Naturally, after Mike and I killed ourselves to switch cameras, Ralphy didn't bother with *his* photography. He was too busy just looking at things.

Or asking questions. When the rest of the class moved to another hallway, Ralphy decided to stop a museum guard.

"Mister," Ralphy whispered to him, "I don't get it."

The air around us even smelled quiet. With the high ceilings and the smooth, almost glistening waxed floor, any sounds you made seemed like sonic booms.

Mr. Evans had warned us to be on our best behavior. Museums like this one, he had said, are world famous. Patrons of the arts come from everywhere to view the displays. We shouldn't even *threaten* to disturb their pleasure in absorbing the works framed on the walls.

For the most part, we were quiet. First of all, people two hundred feet away gave you a dirty look if your stomach growled. Second of all, there was so much to look at. Statues, paintings, and even some weird things we didn't know what to call.

It was sophisticated, for sure. Which made it worse that I was carrying Joel's teddy bear. But the last thing I wanted in this place was Joel on the loose. So I dangled the teddy bear in one hand and pretended it was the most normal thing in the world to do. Even with all the people in suits widening their eyes and looking down their noses at me with a little smile.

"You don't get *what*, little man," the guard said to Ralphy with a sniff.

Wrong person to ask, Ralphy, I thought to myself. It was just a feeling. The guard looked too precise. Not a single wrinkle on his uniform. He even had ironed creases down his sleeves. His hair was blond and cut short, and it was slicked back perfectly. He had a tiny mustache and a long pointed nose, and he wasn't much taller than Mike.

"These paintings," Ralphy continued, pointing at abstract ones by an artist whose signature we couldn't read. "What are they of?"

"Of? Of? What are they of?" The guard sniffed even louder.

One thing about Ralphy. He's so sweet, he never realizes when other people aren't.

"Right," Ralphy said. "There are lines and squiggles and blotches, but I can't understand a single painting. Why can't they paint things people recognize?"

The guard stamped one tiny foot against the floor, and his face turned red.

"*These* artists are masters. They don't need a reason for the way they express themselves. My word, your type of attitude is frustrating."

Ralphy dropped his head.

"I thought museums were for learning," I protested in sudden anger. "How can you learn unless you ask questions?"

"Teddy bears in one hand and stupidity on the other," the guard replied as his eyebrows worked daintily.

Mike's nostrils flared. "In other words," Mike said, "you don't get what the paintings mean, either."

"I beg your pardon!" The guard's voice squeaked in excitement. "This is *intolerable*!"

"So is picking on my friends," Mike said calmly.

"Where is your group leader?" the guard demanded. "We'll see what he has to say about your lack of respect! In the Museum of Modern Art, no less!"

What a sinking feeling. Trouble with Mr. Evans.

Then I remembered how my dad once explained abstract art.

"Sir"—I forced myself to say it politely, knowing we were guests in the guard's museum—"I know exactly what you were trying to tell us."

"Oh?" The guard arched his eyebrows.

"This art doesn't have to *mean* anything," I said. "It's what it makes us feel, right? Just like orchestra music. Does a piano piece need to have a meaning? Do people ask what a nice symphony means? No, they just relax and enjoy the way it makes them feel. You were trying to tell us the same thing about the art, weren't you." I paused. "Right, sir?"

Maybe that last *sir* did it. The guard relaxed.

"Yes," he said. Maybe he was filing the explanation in his memory to use as his own sometime. At least it got us out of trouble.

"I'm glad you understood me," he said. "There's hope for you yet."

He sniffed again. "Now catch up with the rest of the little people before I change my mind about reporting you."

Whew.

Then Ralphy did the unthinkable.

"Thank you, sir." He beamed. "Is it okay if I take a photo of you in front of one of the paintings?"

The guard ran his hand back across his slicked hair and smoothed his mustache.

"Certainly, little man. I must admit, I do look good in photos."

I screamed inside, too far away to prevent it. *No, Ralphy, not the trick camera!*

Mike started walking away to leave the disaster area before it happened.

It didn't help.

With his trick camera, Ralphy plugged the museum guard right between the eyes. Water dribbled down the front of his clean, pressed uniform. A huge stain slowly darkened beneath the guard's name tag as he stood there and silently puffed with rage.

Ralphy's mouth dropped. He looked at me and Mike to see if *we* had water pistols in our hands, but we were frozen, as stunned as the guard. In disbelief, Ralphy snapped another photo. This shot hit the guard's nose and sprayed off his mustache.

This was actually the good part.

The bad part was that during all the confusion that followed, Joel disappeared.

Again.

And we couldn't find him.

CHAPTER 9

Mike, Ralphy, and I sat glumly in our hotel room. Even though it was eleven o'clock at night and we had been up since early in the morning, we didn't feel tired.

Joel was gone. He had been missing for eight hours. The last time I had seen him, he was staring wide-eyed in shock at Mike, Ralphy, and me as the guard took us and Mr. Evans into an office for a discussion.

I stared at the phone, hoping it would ring any second with the police telling us Joel had just been found.

There was no doubt this disappearance was serious. The sick feeling in the pit of my stomach told me. The fact that the police were looking told me. And knowing Mom and Dad were flying in tomorrow night if Joel wasn't found also told me.

Strange, how things in life can change so quickly. Fun in Manhattan one minute, stomach-turning fear the next. Joel was lost in New York City. And it had been dark out there for over two hours.

"I want to go look for him," I told Mike and Ralphy. "Even if it means sneaking out of the hotel."

"I don't blame you," Mike said. "But the police are doing the best they can."

"I know, I know. If only the phone would ring this second."

It didn't.

Mrs. Thompson, who had seen everything and was helpless to stop Joel at the time, told us later what had happened while we were in the guard's office. As escort, she had been with the class in the hallway. Suddenly Joel had broken loose to run after us.

"No police for Ricky! Bring back brother!" he had shouted.

Unfortunately, the door to the office was just down the hall from an emergency exit door. In his rush to rescue me, Joel pushed open the wrong door.

Emergency exits mean emergency alarms. As soon as the bells started clanging, Joel jumped and looked around wildly.

I could understand why. We were in the office when the bells hit, and it was so loud and sudden, I nearly had a heart attack. The guard dashed out to see what had happened.

When Joel saw the guard running full tilt, he shrieked and shot straight outside. By the time the guard had made it to the emergency exit, with us following, Joel had disappeared.

If only we hadn't switched cameras with Ralphy, I thought. Joel wouldn't have been out there now, terrified not only that the "police" had me, but terrified he had done wrong because of the clanging bells.

Oh, no! Oh, no, no, no!

"Joel's in worse trouble than we thought!"

My heart pounded in cold, cold panic as I paced the hotel room.

"The police will never find him," I explained. "Not if every single one in the city is looking."

Mike frowned, puzzled. Ralphy stopped his pacing with me.

"He panicked because he thought the guard was the police taking us, right?"

Mike and Ralphy nodded.

"When the alarm bells started clanging, the same guard came running out again. Think! What would that do to Joel?"

Mike's face turned white. "He'd think it was a policeman after him, too!"

I felt even sicker. "Exactly. And that's why he ran! Joel thinks the police are trying to throw him in jail."

"And nobody disappears like Joel," Mike said soberly. "If he doesn't want to be seen, he won't be seen."

I was ready to throw up. In Jamesville, whenever I teased Joel about being a bad boy, I told him the police would toss him in jail and feed him spiders and orange peels. Not very encouraging to a small kid.

He was out there, alone, running away from the only people who could help him. And I hadn't realized it until now, eight hours too late.

"Guys," I said. If my face looked grim, it was because my whole body felt grim. "Joel's only going to appear for people he knows."

I grabbed my jacket.

"All of this is my fault. That means I've got to go out there and look for him. It's the only chance he has."

CHAPTER 10

"Think, Mike, think. If you were Joel, where would you go here?"

I was nervously shifting Joel's teddy bear from my left hand to my right hand and then back again. Maybe, just maybe, I would be able to give it back to him before the night ended.

In the dark, which even the streetlights could barely break, it seemed smart to whisper. A small side door of the museum loomed in front of us. It was the door Joel had used in his panic eight hours earlier. Backtracking seemed like the best thing to do.

"A teddy bear store," Mike said.

"Give your head a shake," I snapped. "It's no time for jokes. This is serious trouble."

Mike looked at me strangely and then nodded. "As serious as it can get." He paused. "Joel's lost. Not only that, we're now runaways ourselves, and if we don't get back to the hotel by nine in the morning, we're dead ducks. It's after midnight, and of all the places to be, we're alone in the middle of New York City. This is major serious trouble. And you know what?"

I scowled.

"Only one thing can make it worse," he continued, not waiting for my answer. "You mad at me and you mad at the rest of the world, instead of you concentrating on finding your brother."

"Who asked you to come along and preach?" I said.

"As if I'm going to let you disappear, too, pal."

For a moment it was hit him or cry. I closed my eyes. *Dear Lord, we all need strength,* I prayed. Then I stopped, realizing what Mike had said. I had to stop thinking about myself. *And please give most of the help to Joel.*

When I opened my eyes, Mike was watching me gravely. The streetlights threw shadows over his face. Hawaiian shirt with bold flowers. A red high-top shoe and a blue high-top shoe. And him determined to share my trouble. Who could ask for more in a friend?

"I hate it when you're right," I said. "Now open that street map and find us a teddy bear store."

Mike grinned.

The map was discouraging. It showed what we could already see in all directions. Block after block of city. The only break was six blocks north of the museum, where Central Park began at Fiftieth Street.

I had a feeling Joel had headed north, but I wanted Mike to confirm it. "Mike, this door is on the east side of the building, isn't it?"

He nodded.

"So if you were a kid wanting to hide in a hurry, would you run in a straight line from the door, or would you go left or right?"

"Hmmm." He looked around. "Straight east means at least a hundred yards to reach anything worth hiding behind. I'd go left or right instead."

"Exactly. Right takes you south, but it's at least twenty seconds of running to disappear into those trees. We reached the door almost as soon as the bells started clanging and saw nothing, so Joel couldn't have gone that way."

"Which leaves north," Mike said.

"You know Joel as well as I do. Remember our Easter egg hunt this year? When he thought that huge bumblebee crawling in the grass was something the rabbit left behind?"

"Yeah." Mike nodded.

The bee had barely fit in Joel's hand before stinging him. Joel didn't scream or say a word.

Mike said, "He just dropped his basket and ran and ran and ran. We didn't know what was going on."

"What else?" I asked, thinking back to that day.

Mike snapped his fingers. "Straight as a ruler in one direction. He ran in blind panic until his legs stopped moving. One direction. It took us five minutes of bike riding to catch up."

I grinned. "And now he hates the Easter Bunny."

Mike snapped his fingers again. "So what you're saying is this probably scared him just as bad. If we can guess which way he started and how much energy he had, we'll have a good idea of where he stopped."

I squinted at the map. "If Joel took off north, Central Park is in his way. It's the ideal spot for him to hide. You know how much he likes the woods back in Jamesville."

Thinking of it gave me a twinge of homesickness, but I shook it off. We had to find Joel.

"And if we were real smart, Mike, we'd ask people along the way if they saw him. It shouldn't be too hard to remember a six-year-old running full blast."

CHAPTER 11

"Yuck," Mike whispered. "Country music."

"It's Travis Tritt. He's not bad," I whispered back. "Besides, do *you* want to tell *him* you don't like his taste in music?"

Him was big. And mean-looking. Gray stubble on his face and a bristly crew cut. A dirty apron barely covered his solid belly as he stood behind the counter.

It was one o'clock in the morning. Ten hours since Joel had bolted.

The glass door of the small diner closed behind us. Streetlights shone in through large, streaked windows. Country music wailed from a jukebox. The big man looked up at us and grunted. We were the only ones in the diner.

"I'd never question his music," Mike said from the corner of his mouth. "I'm scared to even ask him about Joel."

That left the asking up to me. As we walked to the counter, I hid Joel's teddy bear behind my back. "Excuse me, sir, we're looking for my brother, and I wonder if you could help."

The man wiped his countertop with an old rag.

"Coffee," he said. It didn't sound like a question.

"Pardon me?"

"Coffee. Are you drinking coffee."

"No, sir."

"Nobody stays in this diner unless they're patrons. Get it? Patrons. That means you eat or drink here. You wanna stay, you sit. You wanna sit, you order."

He put his hands on his hips. "Is it coffee."

There was a line of round stools in front of the counter. Mike sat down quickly. "Two coffees, lots of cream and sugar."

Sitting, quickly, seemed like a good idea. I joined Mike.

The big man turned his back on us and shuffled to a huge urn.

"Yuck," I whispered, placing the teddy bear on the stool between Mike and me. "I hate coffee."

"So *you* tell him," Mike whispered.

The big man returned with two mugs of steaming coffee. He glanced at the teddy bear.

"My lost brother is six years old," I said. "Wearing a T-shirt like mine, except smaller. Big eyes. And he was probably running like crazy. Did you see him?"

The big man grunted and turned his back on us again. Mike and I looked at each other. The big man shuffled back with another mug of coffee and placed it on the counter in front of Joel's teddy bear.

"Excuse me," I said. "That's a teddy bear. My brother's, actually."

The big man raised one eyebrow.

"Kid, you don't learn good. Nobody stays in this diner unless they're patrons. You wanna stay, you sit. You wanna sit, you order. That"—he pointed at the bear—"is sitting."

"Oh."

There was some silence as the man stared at us.

Mike shrugged and imitated the man's gruff voice. "Instead of sugar, will ya bring honey with the bear's cream? It's how he drinks it. And he can be one mean patron if he doesn't get his way."

The big man frowned. He placed his hands on the counter and leaned forward, stopping his face inches from Mike's. My heart stopped.

Mike gave him a quick, nervous grin.

The big man then stood back and roared a large laugh. "Honey instead of sugar for the bear! You slay me, kid."

The door swung open behind us, letting in the sounds of the city. A siren screamed faintly. The door shut. I glanced back. A dark-haired girl, about our age, quickly walked to the washroom.

"Your kid brother, huh? Lost?" The big man was friendlier now, and his voice boomed. The girl turned around to stare.

I swung my head back to the man behind the counter.

"Yes, sir. He ran away from the Museum of Modern Art this afternoon. We think he was going this way."

"Forget that 'sir' stuff. Call me Hugo. And you're lucky you came to the right place."

"You mean you saw his brother?" Mike got excited.

"Naw. But I keep my ears open. I hear lots in this joint."

"You heard about my brother, uh, Hugo?"

"Not yet. It's a little early. Who are you? Where you from?"

Mike told him.

Hugo nodded. "This city probably seems big. In one way, the way ya see it, it is. In another way, it ain't. This here's a neighborhood. People get to know it pretty good, especially if they live on the streets. Chances are your brother's still somewhere nearby. Lots of street people come in here to warm up, have a coffee. I'll do some asking. If your brother's around, I'll hear about it from them."

"Street people? You mean they live on the street?"

"Where ya been, kid? Of course they live on the street. They got nowhere else to go." Hugo turned his head because the dark-haired girl had taken a stool at the far end of the counter. "Hang on, will ya? Another patron."

I studied her out of the corner of my eye. She was pretty, with a solemn face. Her hair was almost black and very long and straight. Her skin was dusky, like she was Spanish or Mexican. I was too worried about Joel to wonder why a girl our age was out as late as we were. Which turned out to be a mistake.

I sipped on my coffee and nearly burned my tongue.

Then I started thinking about street people. What would it feel like, sleeping in doorways? Or begging for money? And how could that be right, people in fur coats and limousines passing by beggars digging out of garbage cans? Did God care about the situation? Why wasn't He doing anything about it?

I frowned in thought. The dark-haired girl frowned back as she waited for Hugo to bring her a milk shake. I felt my face turn red. I had been staring past her while I was thinking, and she must have thought I was frowning at her.

"Where was I?" Hugo boomed on his return. "Oh yeah. Your lost brother and how street people would help."

Was it my imagination? Was the girl trying to listen?

Before I could decide about the girl, we were interrupted by the door opening again.

Hugo's face split into a wide grin as he looked toward the door. "Hey, Brother Phillip! Good to see you! The usual?"

"You bet, Hugo." The voice behind our shoulders was deep and soft. I peeked back, expecting to see someone handsome and tall and well dressed.

Wrong. At least about the well-dressed part. His pants were made of a rough brown material, and his shirt was frayed at the collar and cuffs of the sleeves. He might have been handsome, except his hair was shaggy and his face was pale and tired under a few days' growth of beard. One of the street people?

Brother Phillip sat on a nearby stool. He nodded at Mike and me.

"Good evening, gentlemen," he said in that comforting voice. "How are you tonight?" He leaned over Mike and gravely shook the teddy bear's paw. "Pleased to meet you," he said to the bear.

The dark-haired girl rose from her stool.

I was about to call out to her. Something told me she was important to finding Joel. Why had she been listening? What did she know? Was she hiding something?

But Hugo stopped me by introducing us to Brother Phillip, and the girl slipped out the door.

"Brother Phillip runs the mission down the block," Hugo said. "He helps a lot of us street people get back to regular life."

Us street people?

Hugo read my mind. "Brother Phillip got me my job here." Hugo grinned. "The Brother's not a bad guy for a preacher."

I stared. A preacher? In those old, almost tattered clothes? No haircut, no shave?

Things seemed to be happening too quickly. As I tried to take it all in, I noticed the girl. She had stopped in front of the window. Staring. When she saw me looking, she quickly turned and ran down the street.

CHAPTER 12

Mike elbowed me.

"... down at the street mission, someone might be able to help you. A lost brother is a terrible thing."

I turned my attention back to Brother Phillip. His gentle eyes searched my face with compassion. How could I ever have doubted, even for a second, that this was a man of God? I reminded myself never to judge people by their appearances.

"Thank you, sir," I said.

His smile became grave. "But tell me, young man, how is it that you two are wandering the streets at this late hour?"

He smiled at Mike. "Despite that crazy bright shirt and the mixed-up running shoes, you're much too well dressed to be street people. Surely your parents must be worried about you, too, as well as the lost boy."

I wanted to lie. He would probably send us back if I told the truth.

Mike said, "If we tell you, will you promise to keep it a secret?"

Brother Phillip shifted his gaze from my face to Mike's. He laughed lightly. "Sorry, I won't be held to blackmail."

Hugo coughed in the silence that followed. He set down a clubhouse sandwich and a milk shake for Brother Phillip.

Suddenly I was hit with love and fear and, most of all, determination. Joel, my brother Joel, needed me.

I took a deep breath and explained my theory about Joel and the police.

"We are the only way of finding him, sir," I said. "And I think if you try sending us back, we'll run from you and keep looking on our own. I'm sorry to sound disobedient."

He chided me gently. "You may think you are the only *human* way of finding him, and you could be wrong there, too."

Brother Phillip closed his eyes to think. Finally he spoke again. "Unfortunately, and I think Hugo will agree, we have no right to hold you prisoner or interfere in any other way. Especially with your brother gone."

He paused to bite into his sandwich, then stopped as if a thought had hit, and placed it back on his plate.

"Okay," he said. "You keep looking. Meet me back at the street mission at six o'clock this morning. It's called the Good Shepherd's Corner. By then, some of the people will be awake. They'll be able to tell us if they saw Joel during the day. They'll also be able to help you look."

"An army of searchers!" Mike said.

Brother Phillip smiled. "Exactly. Until then, I want you protected."

He reached into his coat and pulled out a couple of graying business cards. The corners were dog-eared. On the front, each card had his name and the address of the Good Shepherd's Corner. He handed Mike the cards.

Mike grinned. "Thanks! What a break, running into you here!"

Brother Phillip's eyes twinkled. "Young man, if we both believed in only lucky breaks, it would be a sad, sad way to live."

I wasn't sure, but I thought the twinkle in his eyes remained as he gravely shook our hands good-bye.

CHAPTER 13

"Someone's following us, Mike!"

And Central Park was not a nice place to be with someone following. It was beautiful—even at night in the moonlight it was beautiful—but with the shadows underneath the trees and bushes, and the long, winding paths, it was also creepy.

It was two in the morning, but strangely, we weren't tired. The desperation to find Joel drove away any thoughts of sleep, and if that wasn't enough, there was the fear of being followed through Central Park.

"Don't *say* that!" Mike hissed.

"What, like if I don't mention it, it's not happening?"

"Right."

I shrugged. "Okay, Mike. There is nobody about fifty yards behind us skulking from tree to tree. And *that* nobody hasn't been staying fifty yards behind us for the last five minutes."

Mike ignored me. "Joooooeeeel. Joooooeeeel. Joooooeeeel," he called softy in all directions.

I elbowed him. "Mike, I'm serious."

"So am I. Seriously scared."

"Then let's do something."

"Like run?"

"Except we need to keep calling for Joel. He could be

anywhere nearby."

Mike sighed. "I've been ready to run for the last twenty minutes. Which is as long as we've been followed. But he's been keeping his distance, so I didn't mention it. The thing is, we need to be able to run if he moves any closer. Got it?"

"Twenty minutes? You knew we were being followed!"

Mike sighed with sarcasm. "My friend, Sherlock Holmes. Now that you know about the guy, walk backward and keep watching for him to make a move. I'll walk in front of you and call for Joel."

We tried that. But I kept losing Mike. Once I hit a tree. I thought I heard a giggle, but I wrote that off to my hypersensitive imagination.

To make the system work, we tried to keep our shoulders together as Mike walked forward and I walked backward.

"Jooooeeeel. Joooooooeeeeel. Joooooooeeeeel."

I kept a sharp eye on the man far behind us who darted from bush to bush. It wasn't going to take much for me to give the warning to run.

After stumbling over Mike's feet for the twelfth time, I stopped. "What was that?!"

"What was what?"

"I thought I heard someone laugh nearby. Did you?"

"Get serious," Mike said. "Are we still being followed back there?"

"Yes. But he's rotten at it. He jumps from tree to tree like we're blind."

"We've got to keep looking," Mike said. "And here is as good as anywhere until the street mission opens. Joel could be anywhere, and we won't find him by running away."

Wonderful.

We started our awkward shuffling again. This time I tripped over Mike's feet and fell. He laughed. Did I hear an echo?

I looked around carefully before getting up.

"Very funny." I handed him one paw of the teddy bear. "You hold that while I hold this end. That way I'll know where you're going without having to bump into you or any trees."

It worked fine. But as soon as we started moving, I heard another giggle. This time I heard it distinctly. So did Mike. A snickering giggle from behind a bush about ten yards away.

Who else was following us? What was happening? I felt in my pocket for the card Brother Phillip had given me. Would it be enough?

Then, scared or not scared, the thought of someone laughing at us made me mad.

I shouted at the bush.

"Show your face, you chicken! Or we're going to come over and get you!"

"Are you nuts?!" Mike hissed.

There was a quivering of the bushes.

Into the moonlight stepped . . . the girl from the diner?

Her face looked as solemn as ever. She stared at us.

Mike and I took three steps closer.

Suddenly, from the corner of my eye, I caught movement to our left. The follower had left the shadows of the trees! He was huge and dressed in a long trench coat with a hat that covered his face, and he was moving toward us at a bumbling trot!

"Aaaaagh! Run for your life!" I yelled.

Mike was gone before I finished shouting. I became a close second and was gaining ground. Running scared does that to me.

CHAPTER 14

My advice to anyone trying to catch two terrified twelve-year-olds is don't wear a trench coat that gets in the way.

We ran through small groves of trees. We ran past ponds. We ran between ducks waddling on the grass in the moonlight, scattering them in all directions. We ran and fell and ran again. We did not stop running until we reached the far edge of the park along Fifth Avenue.

I guess it isn't surprising that by the time we reached the streetlights, there was no sign of the man in a trench coat.

"Next time, Ricky," Mike panted, "speed up a little. With someone chasing us, I don't like slowing down just so you can keep up."

From where I was leaning forward, hands on my knees, gasping, I lifted my head. "Hah!" It was hard to breathe. "Don't you know you're just bait? I keep you around so they'll catch you first and give me time to get away."

Little did I know how true those words would become.

Mike didn't say anything else. He concentrated on getting his breath back.

A street sign on the corner read Fifth Avenue and E. Seventy-sixth Street. According to the address given us by Brother Phillip, we were at least twenty blocks north of the street mission.

"Mike, maybe we should head back to see Brother Phillip."

"It's only two-thirty. He told us to wait until six. What do you expect us to do when we get there?"

"Wait, maybe. Sleep. I don't want to go back into the park, and I don't know what else to do."

The adrenaline of the chase was fading. I began to realize how little hope there was of finding Joel. We were alone in a big city in the middle of the night, and I felt like crying. It was a lousy feeling.

"Good thing that no matter what happens, we have a backup plan," Mike said.

"Great. Wonderful." I had no idea what he was talking about.

"Hey, dummy. Don't you think God can find us here?"

"Huh?"

"Your face is saying you'd rather be at home trying to hide from Joel. So would I. Just remember we have Someone to lean on, okay, pal?"

Backup plan. Our God. Just like Mike not to sound preachy. Just like me to forget at the very moment I should be remembering.

I grinned. "So we'll lean. And walk. The street mission is quite a ways south."

It took even longer than I expected.

Every doorway we passed began to seem inviting.

Finally I said, "You getting tired, Mike?"

"Very."

"Remember," I said, "we have to be back at the hotel by nine o'clock this morning. They'll kill Ralphy for not telling when we left. And it's no fair making everybody worry about us as well as Joel. And if we don't get some sleep beforehand, it'll be a rough day."

It took us five minutes to find a doorway where we could rest.

"I'll stand guard first," I said. I clutched the card Brother Phillip gave me and tried not to notice the shadows around us. "You sleep."

Mike kicked litter out of the doorway and grimaced before lying down.

"Ricky?"

"Yeah?"

"Why were we followed?"

He grinned at giving me the problem, then curled up, using the teddy bear as a pillow. He was asleep before I could say anything.

Guard duty is a lonely task. Mike's question, though, gave me plenty to think about while he slept.

I woke him an hour later.

"They were together," I told him.

"What?" Mike rubbed his eyes and groaned.

"The man and the girl were together. As soon as he saw us moving in on her, he had to run out and protect her. It's the only explanation. She saw us in the diner and knew we were going to be wandering around, so she got the man in the trench coat, and they followed us. Maybe they wanted our money. Who knows?" I was tired. Let him think during his guard duty. "Now *you* figure out why."

The last thing I said was, "Mike, stay awake. We don't have far to go, but we need to be at the mission in an hour."

I settled down and closed my eyes. The fur of the teddy bear tickled my face. *Sleeping in a doorway.* Good thing I was too tired to worry about the hardness of the ground. *How can people live like this? And why should they have to?*

"Boys, boys, ya gotta help me!" It was a tiny old man in a wheelchair. His voice croaked. "You can be rich beyond your dreams if only you help me!"

Mike and I looked at each other. Brother Phillip had left us alone to find some of the people in the mission who might be able to help. We were still a little groggy with tiredness, and a tiny man babbling in a wheelchair was the last thing we expected at the mission.

The walls around us were gray with age. Faded posters of

advertisements added some color. There was a Pepsi-Cola poster so old that the girl carrying the tray of drinks was dressed in the style of clothes I saw girls wearing today. A Goodyear poster had a big, fuzzy white dog peering from behind some tires. There were chewing tobacco posters and motor oil posters and dozens of others. I guess anything looked better than gray walls.

It was a low, flat building. Above us on the second floor, Brother Phillip had explained, were rows of beds where the people slept. Around us, on the main floor, were long tables with folding chairs and a television corner with beat-up stuffed chairs and couches.

Across the main hall was a kitchen. In front were tables set up with plates and cups. We heard clanking and voices as people began to get breakfast ready.

"Well, come here, boys!" The man cackled. "Do ya want to become rich or not?"

CHAPTER 15

The last thing on my mind was money. Joel, definitely. Sleep, maybe. But not money.

Mike and I smiled politely. The man looked crazy.

It didn't stop him from wheeling himself closer in herky-jerky movements. If it bothered him that we had tried to ignore his cackling, he didn't show it.

He had a scraggly gray-and-white beard that nearly reached his belt buckle. The few teeth he did have were crooked and brown. I tried not to breathe through my nose as he crowded us against a table.

"Yes, boys! Rich! All you have to do is become my legs for me!" I had never heard anyone talk faster.

I looked for Brother Phillip. He was nowhere in sight.

"Well? What do you say?" He jutted his beard forward as he pounced on us with the question.

"I, uh . . ." The man made me nervous.

"That's my boy!" The tiny man rubbed his hands together in glee. "I knew you would do it." He dropped his chin and lowered his voice as if he were telling us something important. "Bank robbers and all that." He raised his voice again. "Understand? Been there long time! Long time! Long time!"

He started cackling again and threw his head back.

Where *was* Brother Phillip?

"Yes, boys, secret place. Very secret. Funny too. So, so funny. All those people walking right over it. Don't look! Don't look!"

What weren't we supposed to look at?

"Only takes a token to be rich! Token to be rich!"

Are kids allowed to believe a grown-up is seriously out of his mind? In this case, it felt like the smart thing to do.

Fortunately, Brother Phillip returned. Two rough-looking men trailed behind as he crossed the hall.

"Lyle, Lyle, Lyle." Smiling, Brother Phillip admonished the old man. "These two gentlemen can't become your legs for you. And they want to find a young boy. Not make-believe buried bank money."

Lyle glared at Brother Phillip.

"Hmmph," was all he said. He stuck his tongue out at Mike and me, then spun his chair around and wheeled himself into a corner.

Brother Phillip chuckled. "Lyle's been coming in and out of here since long before even I arrived. Don't take him seriously."

"In and out?" I asked.

A cloud of pain passed across Brother Phillip's face. "If we could do more, some of these people wouldn't have to go out on the streets. Unfortunately, all we can do is give them a place to sleep and barely enough food to get by. They go out during the day and come back nights when they feel like it or when it gets too cold. Some work odd jobs or shine shoes and clean car windows, but some of them are forced to look in garbage cans for bottles or any junk they might sell. Others beg, and, I'm afraid to say, still others steal."

I spoke in a low voice to keep the rough-looking men down the table from hearing. "But how can you let people in if you know they're going out there to steal?"

Brother Phillip shook his head sadly. "At best, we let them know what's right and what's wrong, but we don't push it. Too many questions or too much preaching, and they won't come here for help. And they need it so badly, we don't have the luxury of choosing who's good or bad."

Brother Phillip smiled. "Besides, if God decided to help only the people who deserved it, none of us would pass the test."

That was something I hadn't thought of.

Mike asked, "How does Lyle survive?"

"Begging," Brother Phillip said.

"Begging?" Mike's face looked surprised. "I thought people begged only when they were short money for a cup of coffee or for one meal or things like that."

For the second time a cloud passed across Brother Phillip's face. "I'm sorry to tell you different. Sometimes those are lines they use. A good many of them make a living at it."

"You mean professional beggars?" I said.

"Yes. That's why I'm worried Joel may be more than just lost."

"What!"

"I'll let these two fellows explain." Brother Phillip motioned for the two rough-looking men to join us.

"Hey, dudes." The first man, short with greased-back hair, slouched as he greeted us and looked us over. "Cool bear, man. Wild shirt."

I'd been clutching Joel's bear for so long, I had forgotten it was there. Mike nodded appreciatively at the compliment about his shirt.

"Likewise, dudes." The second picked his teeth as he spoke. He was black, tall and skinny, with hair in a tight Afro. "The Man here tells us you been looking for a runaway."

I nodded and described Joel to them both.

The first one shook his head. "Bad scene. Kid that small sounds too perfect."

"Too perfect?"

"Check out Lyle," the second one said, glancing at the corner where the tiny man was pouting and staring at us. "He's got a wheelchair. People see it, man, they dig a little deeper for spare change. Understand? You start begging and people don't see nothing wrong with you, they go, 'Get a job, bum.' They see the wheelchair, they figure you could use the help."

The first man broke in. "Like, I borrowed Lyle's wheelchair one day, I cleared triple what I do just standing on the corner."

I couldn't help myself. "You used his wheelchair?"

The short one shrugged. "You do what you got to. But the Man—" he grinned at Brother Phillip—"made me see how Lyle needs wheels as bad as I need legs, so I never done it again."

Mike said, "What does this have to do with Joel?"

The second one scratched under his arm for a few seconds before answering. "If you got some kid, eyes as big as saucers, it works major-league better than a wheelchair, dude. Stand on a corner with your hand out and a little kid beside you, people figure you need help real bad."

My voice squeaked with sudden rage. "Somebody would steal Joel to use him as a prop?!"

"I'm sorry, dude." He actually did look sorry. "It's how it works sometimes. What we're gonna do is get our ears down to the ground and see if we can find him. You see . . ." He stopped and shook his head.

I didn't like that at all.

The short one picked up the sentence. "You see, we've been hearing about a bad dude. Not cool bad. Bad as in nasty. Mean Gene Delaney, they call him. The dude's been running a network. Setting up territories."

Trying to understand was almost too much for me. It must have shown on my face.

The second one remained patient. "Territories. Like, he owns some of the prime territory. You start begging on one of his corners or at one of his subway stops, he puts some muscle on you. You go back again, you might find yourself with a broken arm or leg. Word has it, he runs ten or so professionals in this section of town and takes a cut of what they earn. Scary part is, nobody knows where they hole out each night."

I was tired of being dumb, but I had to ask. "Hole out?"

"Yeah. Like the street mission. We come back here. Brother Phillip's cool. So cool some of us make it back to the real world. Like Hugo at the diner. But this bad dude, he takes them all somewhere else. That way the cops can't break the gang. Hides them at night.

Nobody knows where, even though we all know this part of town real good."

"What you're saying," I said slowly, "is my brother got lost and hasn't been found because maybe this Mean Gene Delaney took him to use as a prop for beggars. Each night Joel gets hidden with the rest of the gang and they bring him out during the day for more begging."

Both of them nodded. Brother Phillip placed a gentle hand on my shoulder.

I should have been afraid. But being angry drove it all away.

"If I find even one bruise on my kid brother, Mean Gene is going to be one sorry dude," I said.

This time my face must have shown something different than confusion, because none of them laughed.

CHAPTER 16

"Now it makes sense!" Mike blurted and sat bolt upright in his train seat.

It was seven-thirty Friday morning. Joel had been lost, or stolen, for sixteen-and-a-half hours. We had four stops left before getting off near the Long Island hotel.

My head vibrated as I leaned it against the train window. I didn't care. Anything for a little sleep.

It was a struggle to speak, I was so tired. "Mike, at this point, nothing makes sense."

"Yes, it does. Remember you told me you figured the guy in the trench coat and the girl from the diner were together, and that he started running at us as soon as it looked like we had caught her?"

I sat up, trying to shake off a trance of exhaustion. "I did say that, didn't I?" Guard duty while Mike slept in the doorway had given me too much time to think. "Does it still make sense?"

"Yes! Even more sense now!"

"Keep going," I said. "You're on a roll."

"And just before you fell asleep in the doorway, you told me to figure out *why* they were following us."

Finally I was fully awake.

"If we know why, we'll be a lot closer to Joel!"

Mike nodded. "And I know why. Maybe they are part of

Mean Gene Delaney's gang! Maybe the guy in the trench coat was Mean Gene himself!"

"You're right," I told him. "It fits. She overhears us in the diner. She gets worried we'll find Joel, gets some help, and follows us to make sure we don't get close to Joel."

"Or . . ." Mike's lips tightened.

I understood immediately. "Or they were waiting for the perfect time to nab the both of us."

"Exactly," Mike said.

There was only one thing. What if we were wrong? What if the whole theory was wrong? What if Joel was already a hundred miles away? I blocked it from my mind. We had no choice but to look. It was a slim chance but much, much better than nothing.

We looked out the window, lost in our own thoughts, until the train reached our stop. Neither of us spoke until we were in our hotel room, shaking Ralphy awake, much to his relief.

At 9:05 A.M., I was ready to go crazy. The hotel room around me seemed as tiny as a breadbox. I didn't feel like watching television. I couldn't sleep, even though I was exhausted from the night before.

Joel was out there, somewhere, and I had been told to stay at the hotel and wait for messages from the police. I would stay until tonight, when everybody returned, and then Mike and I could look again for Joel. It was little consolation that most of Brother Phillip's helpers were looking for Joel as I sat on the edge of the bed. I wanted to be out there. I wanted to be doing something, anything, not waiting.

The rest of the group had split into two separate tours for the day. Mr. Evans had said nothing could be done anyway, and it wouldn't help the situation if everybody sat around waiting. So I sat around. Alone.

There was a knock on the door.

Great. They wouldn't even let me suffer in peace. Who could *that* be?

My spirits were so low, I opened the door and walked back to the bed without looking to see.

"Ricky?" It was a soft whisper.

My heart thumped.

Before I could fully turn around to face the doorway, Lisa had wrapped her arms around me, filling my face with her soft long hair.

"I'm so sorry about Joel," she said, holding me tight. "I couldn't let you worry about him alone."

I'm not sure her tight hugging was the part that made it difficult for me to breathe.

I *am* sure that Mike and Ralphy nearly had heart attacks as they walked through the open door and saw Lisa with her arms around me.

Mike rolled his eyeballs. "So much for worrying about having our fearless leader suffer alone all day."

Ralphy giggled.

Lisa ignored them, gave me a final squeeze, and whispered in my ear, "We'll find Joel. Okay?" Then she let go and faced Mike and Ralphy.

"Hi, guys." She noticed their grins. Her return frown nearly sent sparks flying from her eyes. "Wipe those dumb smirks off your faces. Any time things go as rotten for you as they are going right now for Ricky, I'll be happy to give either of you a hug, too. It's called friendship."

We never like making Lisa too mad. While Mike and Ralphy were busy wiping away dumb smirks, I sighed inwardly. Friendship is okay, but with someone like Lisa, once in a while you hope it's a little more. Oh well.

Suddenly the obvious dawned on me. I snapped my fingers. "Hey! Why aren't you guys touring?"

"Easy," Mike said. "We asked Mr. Evans if we could transfer to Mrs. Thompson's group. He said yes, and here we are."

That made sense. Lisa was in that group. "You mean Mrs. Thompson's group decided not to go on tour today?"

Mike grinned. "No, idiot. We didn't say we were *going* to transfer to Mrs. Thompson's group. Just asked if we *could.* We, uh, missed the bus."

"What?"

"At least this way Mr. Evans won't worry about us being gone all day," Mike said. "He thinks we're safely with the other group."

Mike turned his attention to Lisa. "So why are you here?"

Lisa blushed. "Strangely enough, I happened to ask Mrs. Thompson and Mrs. Bradley if I could transfer to Mr. Evans' group." Her blush grew deeper. "I, uh, missed the bus, too."

CHAPTER 17

If you want to do something wrong, you can always find a way to justify it. We told ourselves we were desperate, made ourselves believe that it was okay to leave the hotel and continue the search for Joel.

Wrong. To do it over again, I would do it differently. Get permission. Let the grown-ups know what was happening. But at the time, we blinded ourselves by deciding it was the only way Joel could be rescued.

Which was why we were now about to walk into an abandoned warehouse in some forgotten corner of Manhattan. It was eleven o'clock, twenty hours after Joel had disappeared.

The warehouse was long and low, directly in the center of a large, fenced parking lot. Shattered glass from broken windows covered the cracked asphalt in front of the building walls. Doors leaned crookedly from hinges. Pigeons flew in and out of the shadows.

"Are you sure this is the address Brother Phillip gave us?"

"Yes, Mike."

If Mean Gene could live in there, he was meaner than I cared to know. I frowned. "Do you feel like we're being followed?"

"Don't say things like that!" He frowned back. "You

always imagine things, and you know it."

He was probably right. I do expect the worst most of the time. It's the result of having a brother as terrifying as Joel. A brother I wanted back badly.

But I wasn't going to let Mike win the argument that easily. "So am I imagining how scary that warehouse looks?"

Lisa, standing beside us in the sunshine, shuddered. "No," she said. "I'm glad we called Ralphy with the address."

Ralphy was our backup. He was staying at the hotel while we searched for Joel. We had to call him every half hour with our location. The rule was we could miss one call. If he didn't hear from us within a half hour of missing one call, he would phone the police and report us as missing, giving them our last known location.

It sounded like a system in a spy novel, which is where I got the idea from, but we had no idea where the chase for Mean Gene Delaney's gang of professional beggars would lead us, and it seemed like our only protection.

After our reunion in the hotel room, we had first taken the train back into Manhattan, then a subway to the Good Shepherd's Corner. Brother Phillip told us most of his people were already on the street, looking for Joel. He told us our job was to check out the warehouse, to look for signs showing it had been used as a hideout.

There we stood. Mike had not bothered to change shirts from the night before. I was still stuck carrying a teddy bear that belonged to the brother I so badly missed. Lisa, hair swirling slightly in the breeze, looked cool and confident. We all stared at the warehouse.

All my tiredness was gone. "No time like now, huh?"

They both nodded. We marched forward. Boldly marching or not, I still couldn't shake the feeling that we were being followed.

The door creaked open, a sound effect I would gladly have missed. Beams of sunlight poked into the center of the building, leaving the corners much too dark.

I reached for Lisa's hand to keep her from being frightened.

"What's the deal?" Mike asked in the dark. "Do you want to kiss me next?"

CHAPTER 18

We took twenty steps farther into the warehouse. Exactly twenty steps. It was the kind of place where you went slow and counted steps. And each step seemed to take five minutes. It was enough to make you wish you were stupid enough to smoke—at least you could burn matches to break the darkness.

"Nothing." Mike finally broke the silence.

"What do you mean, 'nothing'?"

"Nothing here. Absolutely nothing here. I'm sure of it. So let's go."

I wanted to agree. The dust was thick in the air, making the sunbeams that broke into the middle of the huge warehouse seem like a frantic dance of the insane.

Then, below our level of clear hearing, there was a scurrying. Or was it my imagination? Every time we stopped, there was solid, unyielding silence. When we started moving again, that undercurrent of movement would rustle at the edges of our hearing.

My skin crawled.

"Tell me you dropped Joel's teddy bear," Lisa said. "I feel something furry."

"I'm sorry, I can't tell you that." I was clutching it hard enough to break into the stuffing.

"I was afraid of that," she said. Dimly, I could see her

kick something on the ground in front of her. "This is the last time I wear open-toed sandals."

Her voice stayed calm as she continued. "A dead rat," she said. "I hate rats. I hate dead rats worse."

"Rats?! Rats?!" Mike screamed and ran to the sunlight in the middle of the warehouse.

Wisely, I refrained from commenting on his cowardice. Good thing, because something tickled my foot. And then came back and tickled it again. Ten seconds later I was right beside Mike, happy to be in what little sunshine we could find. It wasn't exactly a quiet moment. People will do these things after live rats run over their feet.

Mike and I might have stayed there forever, hugging each other in the sunbeam and jumping up and down and yelling to keep the rats away, except the lights went on.

We slowly let go of each other.

"Oh," Mike said. "Hi, Lisa."

I could only grin a stupid grin.

She was standing at the side of the warehouse, her hand on the light switch, shaking her head at us.

The rats, of course, had disappeared. There were plenty of places for them to go. Stacks of splintered lumber lay in all directions, as if somebody had started dismantling the interior and given up halfway through. Empty cardboard boxes were strewn at all angles. There was even a huge pile of rags halfway between Lisa and the two of us. But no sign of beggars living there. And no sign of Joel.

Lisa started walking toward us.

"I was going to tell you about that light switch—" Mike began. I elbowed him. No sense in making us look even dumber. Especially in front of Lisa.

"I can't see anything here," I told her. "We should probably report back to Brother Phillip that this was a dead end."

Lisa nodded. Then, just as she reached the pile of rags, it began to move. From the depths, a man stood!

His eyes were sunk deep into a horribly scarred face. His clothes were draped over his body like the rags from which he was rising. I couldn't picture a worse monster of a human being. And he was reaching outward! Lisa was frozen in terror.

It wasn't something I wanted to do. But my body took over and ignored the fear in my brain. I grabbed a heavy wooden slat from the stack of lumber beside me.

"Aaaaagh! Aaaaagh!" The war cry came unbidden from the pit of my stomach and I charged toward them, as shocked to be doing it as I was to see the horrible creature clutching toward Lisa.

Lisa stepped back as I charged into the pile of rags, and my shoulder rammed the man in the ribs. He fell backward. I fought to keep my balance, then turned and brought the wood above my head, ready to smash as hard as I could. Anything to keep us safe.

"No! No! Please, no!" The frailness of his voice was like a slap across my face.

He shielded his face with a skinny arm. That's when I saw he was almost bones and rags. The horrible scars were only streaks of dirt. And the eyes sunk deeply into his face were filled with pleading.

I lowered the wood.

Mike and Lisa stood behind me.

"You were reaching for her," Mike accused.

The man dropped his arm and shook his head sadly. "No. No. I was reaching to keep from falling. Sometimes, if I haven't eaten, it makes me faint to stand up."

It was obvious what we had to do next.

"Cough it up, Mike."

He grinned, reading my mind. "Cough what up?"

"The chocolate bar you've been hiding from me all morning."

"Oh. That."

Mike handed the skinny man the chocolate bar I had seen him buy and stuff into his jacket pocket at the subway concession stand.

Lisa opened her purse and found a small package of cookies they had served us for dessert on our flight to New York City. How some girls manage not to eat stuff right away is beyond me. She placed the cookies on the rags beside the man.

"It's not much," I said. "But we weren't expecting company."

The gaps in his teeth showed as he smiled at my attempt to joke.

For nearly a minute, there was only the sound of a hungry man eating. He was not polite about it. We all looked away to ignore the greedy smacking of his lips and the crumbs smudging his grimy hands.

Manhattan was not what I had expected it to be. The ugliness and dirtiness and the uncaring hurriedness made me feel vaguely ashamed, as if being part of mankind put part of the blame on me. And I couldn't understand how God, who was supposed to be Love, let all of this happen.

"Why?" I blurted suddenly.

He must have guessed what I meant, because he looked down at his rags and his skinny, dirty body and said in a dull voice, "Why not?" Then he laughed bitterly, as if feeling sorry for himself gave him energy. "Kid, go ahead. Wrinkle your nose at the way I smell and look. You fall this far, and it don't matter anymore. The way you're dressed, you got a mommy and daddy"—he sneered at that—"who make sure everything is proper for you. Well, some of us never started with a mommy and daddy"—the sneer again—"and just learned not to bother trying. So you end up feeling and looking way older than you are, and it just don't matter. Nothing matters."

Still, he looked scared, as if he didn't believe himself.

"I'm sorry," I said.

"Don't bother." His sudden energy drained. "You all done good with the food. It's more than most people give me." He frowned. "Why are you kids here, anyway?"

"We're looking for my kid brother. He belongs to this teddy bear. He got lost or stolen yesterday."

The man squinted. "Fair enough. I wish I could help, but I don't know nothing about it. Why this old warehouse?"

Mike said, "We're looking for the guy who may have stolen him."

"The guy who stole him?"

"Mean Gene Delaney," Mike answered.

The skinny man shrunk into himself. "Mean Gene Delaney," he whispered. "Here? Not here!"

"You know about him?"

The man shook his head vigorously. "Nothing, Nothing."

We all knew he was lying.

"Okay," he finally admitted. "You'll never find him to tell him you heard it from me anyway. It happened like this. I was down in the subway once. My regular spot, hat on the ground in front of me. Average day for begging. Then this guy in a trench coat—"

Trench coat! Mike and I shot startled glances at each other.

"—stops and grabs my arm. He twists it until I'm standing, and still he twists it until I figure it's broken for sure. Then he tells me to take off and never come back. Only Mean Gene's people get the subway stations, he says. If I come back, he tells me, he'll yank my arm that extra half inch and break it for sure. And he tells me if I come back after that, he'll break my leg and set me in front of a subway train. Then—"

The man's face twisted in fear and disbelief. "Then he hops onto the subway track and starts walking. A minute later a train comes through from his direction. I figure for sure I'll see him spread across the front of the train. Nothing. The guy just vanished into thin air. And I never went back."

I wasn't sure how much to believe. "What subway station?"

He shook his head. "Mean Gene would track me down."

"You have to tell us! It's my brother!"

He shook his head again.

"You don't like it here," I said. "Now imagine you're a little kid and you're away from home. Please, please help him."

The homeless man closed his eyes. And sighed. "Broadway and West Fifty-fifth."

That was one stop before the exit we had been using each time into Manhattan!

The man's voice was tired as he sank into the rags. "Now go away. Beat it. Leave me alone."

Mike said, "Can't we help?"

The man laughed in disgust. "Sure, wave a magic wand and make the world better, kid."

The bum was old and ugly when he felt sorry for himself.

"Which door, Mike?" I wanted out as soon as possible.

Mike shrugged. "Side door. It's quicker." He felt the same way I did.

We left the man sitting in his pile of rags.

It made me feel better when Lisa stopped me in the sunshine just outside. "Thanks for the protection," she whispered. "Even if I didn't need it after all." As Mike was walking away, she gave me a kiss on the cheek. It tingled for a long time.

CHAPTER 19

Things would have been very different had we decided to leave by the front entrance. Instead, we slipped out the side, with our usual laughter and joking around reduced to quietness by what we had seen inside.

We rounded the corner of the warehouse, in a silence that saved us, and saw what had been waiting for us at the front door. A street gang!

Ten, maybe fifteen members. All I saw was slick black ponytailed hair, gleaming muscle, and blue tattoos under ripped T-shirts, and bicycle chains in every hand.

Each of them was staring intently at the front door. From where we stopped in shock at the corner, it was less than a whisper's distance to their backs and shoulders. One turn of one head in the gang, and they would spot us!

Lisa, Mike, and I knew better than to even breathe loud. We started tiptoeing backwards.

If I had thought each step in the dark warehouse took forever, I soon learned how it felt stretched even longer. One scuff on pavement, one click of stone, and we would be spotted. Unless we reached the gate at the edge of the parking lot, there was no way we could outrun a healthy street gang.

Step by step we moved backward. The distance to the gate was only half a football field away, but it seemed like walking to the moon.

Finally we were far enough away to whisper.

"Lisa, there's a chain and a rusty lock at the gate. Once we get through, you run. Mike and I will pull the gate shut and hope the lock works."

"Is the fence high enough?" Mike whispered.

I took a quick glance at the wire meshing of the fence.

"We better hope so, pal."

It was, and the lock worked. Everyone in the street gang heard a loud creak as we pulled the old gate shut, and they started running, but by then it was too late.

The rusty lock snapped into place, and they were locked in!

"Run, Mike!"

He was gone before I finished his name.

I took my first step and fell! The bottom of my pants had snagged on the wire mesh. I stood and yanked. The sound of ripping jeans had never seemed so sweet. Then I stopped.

It was the dark-haired girl. Her dusky skin and sharp cheek bones were unmistakable. She was leading the pack!

At first I barely believed my eyes. Then I didn't believe my ears.

"Reeeecky! Wait!"

Was that her calling? How did she know my name?

"Reeeecky! Reeeeecky!"

I might have stayed to find out how she knew, trusting the fence to keep me safe, and hoping to trust her, but I saw, behind all of them, another person step out of the front entrance of the warehouse.

The man in the trench coat! His hat put his face into shadow. Mean Gene Delaney. He must have gotten my name from Joel. So she got my name from him! They were together, just like Mike and I had guessed!

I bolted.

"Excuse me, sir," I said. "Can you spare a fellow some loose change?"

"How about a loose set of knuckles, kid? Right in the nose." The gruff man had his wife clutching his arm as they walked through the subway station.

"I prefer change, sir."

"Oh, George, quit being so mean. Give the poor kid some money."

"So he can buy another teddy bear? I hate that cutesy stuff from beggars. Forget it." He pulled her along the platform.

"Sometimes, George, I could just slap you. . . ." Their arguing trailed off as they walked away from me to step onto a subway train.

It was past noon. Joel had been gone for more than twenty-one hours. Back in Jamesville, I would have given a half-year's paper route money to be safe from Joel for that long. Here in New York, I was ready to do anything to see him again.

Which is why I was begging in the subway station at Broadway and West Fifty-fifth Street.

It had taken some convincing for Mike and Lisa to agree to my plan. I told them that Brother Phillip and his people were already looking on the streets, and I didn't think three more searchers would help, especially if those three knew as little about Manhattan as we did. So I had suggested we try a different angle.

I would beg, and wait for Mean Gene or one of his people to capture me.

Simple, right? All except for the begging.

Mike and Lisa were watching from a safe place. If someone kidnapped or threatened me, they would follow until they discovered Mean Gene's hideout. Then they would get help and rescue Joel and me.

We had decided the best place to start was the station where that poor man in the warehouse had been threatened: Broadway and West Fifty-fifth.

I sat with my back to the tiled, curving walls of the subway platform. Trains came and went roughly every two minutes. I couldn't time it for sure—I had stuffed my watch in my pocket so that people wouldn't think I had much money. My shirt was also untucked, and my hair was as messy as I could make it. Mike's hat was on the platform floor in front of me to hold any money I collected.

Hundreds of people rushed on and off each train. Most of them ignored me. I had Joel's teddy bear sitting beside me. If he were ever nearby, he would spot the bear first.

"Excuse me—"

I didn't get a chance to finish. Another person stepped over me as if I didn't exist.

Some people gave money without looking. Some snarled at me. A few stopped and smiled before dropping some change. One creepy man said he had some chocolate bars in his car. I smiled and told him I was an undercover cop, and he left as if I had jabbed him with a stun gun.

"Spare change? Spare change for a hungry kid?"

Clank. Clank. A few more coins hit the hat.

Before I knew it, I was sniffing in disdain when people dropped pennies. I nodded politely at dimes and nickels. And I beamed at paper money.

What was happening to me? Was this how easy it was to give up and depend on the charity of strangers?

I imagined what it would be like to have no parents, no home, nothing to care about. Thousands of strangers, nobody caring. Me giving up and not caring. Then sinking into a life of just finding enough to eat and only worrying about a place out of the rain to sleep. I began to understand a life of desperation.

But I still didn't know why so much suffering would happen to so many people. Surely God cared, didn't He?

Look at the fur coat on that beautiful woman, will you? She's loaded, I'm sure. "Just a little change, ma'am. Help out me and my brother."

She turned her nose up at me.

I stuck my tongue out at her receding back. *Probably fake fur and she's fat underneath it anyhow.*

I caught the tone of my thoughts and I rubbed my eyes and gave my head a shake. *Mean Gene had better come by soon and kidnap me,* I thought. *Otherwise, I'll probably go crazy.*

He didn't. Nothing. Not for over two hours. Before I knew it, it was already three o'clock, the deadline Mike and Lisa and I had decided for my time as bait. All we could do now was go to the mission and hope Brother Phillip had news about Joel. Then it was back to the hotel before Mr. Evans and Mrs. Thompson discovered we were missing.

Three o'clock. Exactly twenty-four hours without Joel.

The shortness of time remaining suddenly felt like a collar around my throat. We had to find Joel.

I straightened suddenly. With the desperation, I felt anger, too. This city was not going to beat us.

CHAPTER 20

"Kid, are ya sure ya want another three dogs?"

"Loaded, man. Cheese, chili, ketchup, mustard, even onions. Anything you have in your cart, just throw it on them dogs." Mike said it with a grin. "My buddy's picking up the tab. And we need more Coke, too."

I could afford it. My pockets were bulging with change from a couple hours of begging. We had stopped counting at twenty dollars—even after spending money on ten hot dogs between the three of us.

I could not believe how good the hot dogs tasted.

We were on the street just down from the mission. Joel was definitely the most important thing on my mind, so important that I had hardly touched my breakfast. Then the aroma of fresh-cooked hot dogs coming from a cart on the sidewalk reminded my stomach.

"Anything for the teddy bear, Mr. Big Spender?" the hot dog vendor asked.

"Good one," I said, tired of all the teddy bear comments after hours of begging with it beside me. "Are those raw hot dogs that alley cat is pulling from underneath your cart?"

The man dropped his tongs and scrambled to his knees to look. Mike and Lisa and I hurried down the sidewalk to the mission before he could get back to his feet again, gulping our hot dogs as we went.

We were hoping for news from Brother Phillip. Without it, I didn't know what to do next.

The first person we saw in the mission was Lyle, who, Brother Phillip had told us, rarely left these days. He looked at us briefly and looked away, as if he knew there was no use trying to get us to believe his story.

It made my heart twinge with sadness to see his tiny face and beard almost lost within the wheelchair. His eyes were dull and his chin sagged into his chest. That killed me, thinking he was out of hope for the day.

Brother Phillip was at the far end of the room, squatting to speak to someone in a chair. He hadn't seen us. It gave me enough time to visit Lyle.

"Lyle, I've got a very important job for you," I said, not sure that I wanted him to know I felt sorry for him. "And I can only pay you this much money."

I dumped the rest of the begging proceeds into his lap. Then I looked for an excuse to pay him. "I, uh, need you to keep your ears open for anything on a kid who's been lost for a couple of days. He's my brother and I want him back. Is that enough pay?"

Lyle started cackling quietly. "'Nuff. 'Nuff. More than 'nuff. Get you brother back. For sure. For sure."

I saw his crooked dirty teeth as he grinned from ear to ear, and I felt better. At least all that begging hadn't been a total waste.

Brother Phillip saw us and waved frantically.

We hurried closer and saw that he was applying a wet white rag to the head of the short, greasy-haired man who first told us about Mean Gene Delaney. When Brother Phillip pulled the rag away, it was soaked red with blood!

"What happened?"

"Good and bad," Brother Phillip said. The man's forehead was knotted with a huge purple bruise, cut in the middle and still bleeding.

Brother Phillip said to the man in the chair, "Is it feeling better?"

The man nodded and winced.

"It looks all bad to me," I said.

The man winced a tight grin. "Not all bad, dude. I saw your brother."

Electricity shot through my arms and legs. "What? You saw Joel! Is he okay? Where is he? Did you get him? Tell me—"

"Easy, son," Brother Phillip said. "Your brother is okay. We don't have him, but about twenty of us are out there looking for him."

Joel was nearby! All the guesses had been right! We hadn't been wasting our time by looking in this area. The relief of newfound hope flooded me.

The man in the chair groaned. "It's like this. I'm walking down the street and I see this blind beggar. He's got these dark round glasses and a white cane on the sidewalk in front. Then I notice the kid. Only he's tied to the beggar. Like if I was blind and needed my kid along, it only makes sense. You can't have no kid walking away when you're blind and can't find him, right?"

We nodded. Brother Phillip gently wiped the man's forehead.

"Then I'm thinking, what if it ain't Joel? All I got to work on is your description. No picture. No nothing. So I walk up. I know the blind man can't see me. I stand there and ask real fast, 'You Joel?' The kid nods. So I'm thinking this is gonna be like taking candy from a baby, robbing a blind beggar. I go to untie the rope and bam! This cane hits me from nowhere! Right across my head! Accurate? You bet. You guys know Dan Stubbing? Yankee player, hit a grand slam yesterday? *He* could take batting lessons from this guy."

Just when Mike had forgotten all about how sore he was about not being invited into the clubhouse.

The man groaned and continued. "Get this. The blind man stands, grabs the kid, and runs down the sidewalk. He's like a full-back dodging tackles, I tell ya. In and out of the crowd like a knife through butter. I'm saying to myself, if that dude's blind, the sun ain't gonna rise in the east tomorrow. By the time I get back to my feet, they're both gone. Zip. Right down the stairs. Subway city, dude. And I know I ain't gonna get them then. So I notice the blood messing up my shirt and I come straight here to Brother Phillip."

I was distracted by a hand going into my back pocket.

Lyle had rolled up behind us. His little claw of a hand was pushing something into my pocket.

"For you! For you! Be nice to Lyle, Lyle be nice to you! Take. Okay? Take."

I tried to hide my irritation. "Sure, Lyle. Thanks."

I turned my back on him. "But you saw Joel? He looked fine? He's in the area and we can find him?"

Brother Phillip nodded. "Just give us a little time."

That was all I could think about. How little time there was.

CHAPTER 21

"Once Ricky heard about Joel, it was all we could do to get him back here," Mike said to Ralphy in the hotel room, motioning his head at me as I sagged into a chair. "Nothing's going to stop him from going back down to Manhattan tonight."

"I'm going with you guys, then," Ralphy announced. "It was bad enough I had to stay and wait for you all day. I barely made it through the phone call with your parents."

"They called?!"

"Yes." Ralphy sighed. "You were so full of news about Joel, I forgot to mention it. They won't be here until tomorrow afternoon. The plane had mechanical problems and their flight was delayed. When they get here, they'll stay waiting for the police to find Joel while the rest of the class goes back to Jamesville."

"The police *can't* find Joel! You know that!"

"So was *I* going to tell them that? They sounded so worried about everything. I told them you were just fine, and as I said it, I was praying you were."

Poor Ralphy. The most nervous one of us having the hardest job.

My decision was easy. And later, I was very glad for it.

"Mike, we'll take him."

"But what if Mr. Evans checks our room?"

"At this point, it won't make any difference. We've only got tonight. If we find Joel, I won't care how much trouble we're in. If we *don't* find Joel, I'll care even less about trouble back at the hotel."

"True enough. And Lisa?"

I thought about the cool way she had found the lights in the warehouse while Mike and I were dodging rats. I also thought about that little kiss on my cheek. I said, "I think she'll feel better to be helping, too."

So it was settled.

That night, the four of us escaped the hotel by a side entrance. We left Joel's teddy bear at the hotel. He had been missing for thirty-one hours, the longest hours of my life. I prayed we would be returning him to his teddy bear tonight. No matter how little sleep I got.

"Country music," Lisa whispered as we stepped into the diner. The four of us had split up. For lack of any better plan, Mike had decided he and Ralphy would hang around the subway station where I had begged earlier in the day. They would wait and watch for any sign of Joel while Lisa and I stopped at the diner and the street mission for news. Since the diner was on the way, and it was the night shift for Hugo, we had decided to see if he had heard anything.

Lisa squinted one eye in thought at the jukebox. "That sounds like Travis Tritt."

"Bingo," I replied. "And remember, you don't need to be nervous about Hugo."

Hugo grinned his big meaty grin as we approached the counter.

"This is my friend Lisa," I said and watched as they shook hands. "Two vanilla milk shakes, please." I had learned from our first visit to the diner. Why order coffee when you aren't going to drink it anyway?

"Coming right up, patrons," he said. "I heard that Duke seen your brother."

I nodded. So that was the short, greasy-haired man's name that had given us the news.

Hugo continued, "I also heard Duke got nailed good across the head by a blind man. He ain't never gonna live that one down. Especially since he let them get away down the subway."

Something clicked. Subway. Duke's words came back to me. *"By the time I get back to my feet, they're both gone. Zip. Right down the stairs. Subway city, dude . . ."*

I snapped my fingers. "That's right. He *did* say subway."

Hugo shrugged.

"But Lyle interrupted us and I didn't think anything of it at the time," I said, trying to decide what was suddenly nagging at my mind.

"Lyle? Wheelchair Lyle?" Hugo asked. "I'm surprised he didn't flip out when Duke mentioned that. Lyle hates the subway. Swears never to go there again."

Hugo turned to get the milk shakes for us. Hearing about Lyle reminded me that I had not even bothered to see what he had stuffed into my pocket. Joel, and Duke's news of Joel, had been much more important at the time.

I reached back and pulled out a wadded newspaper clipping. Little did I know what a difference it would have made had I changed jeans at the hotel because of ripping them on the fence in the morning. Because then the clipping would still be in the hotel—and Mike and Ralphy could have been lost forever, along with Joel.

Hugo returned. I sucked on the milk shake as I glanced at the clipping.

BANK ROBBER DISAPPEARS INTO THIN AIR

Heist Yields a Hundred Thousand

City police are still scratching their heads after failing to apprehend a single man who walked into First Bank National this afternoon and calmly held the tellers at gunpoint.

> Police spokesmen say the man left on foot and to all appearances was certain to be caught. . . .

"Why does Lyle hate the subway, Mr. Hugo?" Lisa asked politely to fill the silence as I read.

Hugo shook his head. "Poor Lyle. It happened so long ago, only a few of us old-timers remember. Makes sense, too, if you think about it. Lyle's in a wheelchair because he got hit by a subway train."

I only half heard Hugo, because the nagging in my mind became a shrieking of alarm bells. *Subway.* There it was again. *Subway.* The man in the warehouse being threatened at Broadway and West Fifty-fifth. Then the blind man's getaway with Joel. Now Lyle.

But there was more! Something I had heard about the subway that was now important! I could feel it! But what was it?!

Hugo shook his head. "We still can't figure it out, you know. Sure, people fall off the platform and get hit. Sad, but it happens. That's not the way it happened to Lyle. He's way down the tunnel. Walking. You got to be crazy to walk down the tunnel. That's where he got hit. And he won't tell anybody what he was doing that far from the platform."

Something caught my eye in the newspaper article, and the alarm bells became sirens in my head. Trying to remember the phrase that tied all of this together bothered me so much that I had to stand and begin pacing. Hugo and Lisa stared at me.

What had I heard before that mattered so much to all of this? Then it hit me. *The man in the warehouse! Yes, yes, yes!*

I took a deep breath. Hugo's answer to my next questions could not be more crucial.

"Hugo. You say only a few old-timers remember. And you're one of them, right?"

He nodded. My heart was beating so hard that a low roar filled my ears.

I looked at the date on the newspaper clipping.

"He was hit in 1959, right?"

Hugo nodded again, and his eyes grew wider.

"And it was the West Broadway and Fifty-fifth station." I spoke slowly and deliberately, with the low roar threatening to take away my breath. "Lyle had walked down the tunnel at West Broadway and Fifty-fifth. That's where the train hit him."

Hugo's large forehead wrinkled as he frowned in amazement.

"How did you know all that?"

It was now blazed across my mind, the way the man in the warehouse had twisted his face in fear and disbelief as he sat in that pile of rags, giving us the phrase that had made everything click.

". . . then he hops onto the subway track and starts walking. A minute later, a train comes through from his direction. I figure for sure I'll see him spread across the front of the train. Nothing. The guy just vanished into thin air. . . ."

Everything fit because of it. The newspaper article. Lyle in a wheelchair. Why the subway kept cropping up. And Mean Gene Delaney.

I didn't dare waste time explaining. I could always get back to Hugo later. Joel was missing and I knew where he was. And Mike and Ralphy were in terrible danger.

"No time, Hugo. Sorry!"

I grabbed Lisa's wrist to pull her away from the milk shake. She recognized my urgency as I threw money on the counter.

"We have to run and run hard!" Hugo never heard the last part of that sentence. I was out the door at full speed before I finished speaking. Lisa was right at my heels.

I wished we had time to stop so I could explain everything to Lisa. But we didn't. We tore along the sidewalks and almost crashed through the doors of the street mission, we were running so hard.

It was ten-thirty. Thirty-one-and-a-half hours since Joel had disappeared. The lights in the mission were dim as people settled for the evening.

I spotted Duke resting on a chair in front of the television.

I almost shouted. "Brother Phillip! Where's Brother Phillip?"

Duke jumped.

"Huh? He's following—" Duke stopped himself short, but I was too excited to think anything of it. "The Man's out. I don't know where."

"Lyle, then! I need Lyle!"

"Asleep upstairs."

"You *have* to bring him here. It's more important than you can imagine!"

I was almost certain I was right. Lyle would confirm it. He would give me the final answers I needed. I shuddered to think about what might have happened if I hadn't given him the hatful of begging money to help find Joel.

Duke saw the intensity in my eyes and didn't protest. "Yeah. Sure. I'll get him for you."

While we waited, I paced. Lisa watched me with interest but didn't say anything.

"Two more minutes, Lisa," I replied to her questioning eyes. "You'll know everything in two more minutes. And then I pray we're not too late."

I pulled the newspaper clipping out of my pocket and reread it. What was that Lyle had first cackled to Mike and me?

"*... Bank robbers and all that ... Yes, boys, secret place. Very secret. Funny too. So, so funny. All those people walking right over it. Don't look! Don't look! ... Only takes a token to be rich! Token to be rich!*"

It made more sense now, I told myself. He wasn't telling Mike and me not to look, he meant that the people walking over it are the ones who don't look. And "token" must mean—

"Here he is, kid. And let me tell ya, he ain't real happy about being woke up."

Lyle rubbed his eyes with gnarled hands and focused his bleary eyes on Lisa and me.

"I'm going to talk to you about the present you put in my pocket this afternoon," I told him. "Do you want Duke here to be listening?"

I had guessed right. Lyle quickly shook his head sideways.

Duke grumbled but went back to his chair in front of the television.

It didn't seem nice to tower over the tiny man in his wheelchair, so Lisa and I pulled chairs away from a nearby table and sat.

I stared directly into his eyes.

"Lyle, I want you to tell me how to get into Mean Gene Delaney's hideout."

CHAPTER 22

Terror flickered in his eyes, but it seemed there was some relief, too. If my guesses were right, that, too, made sense.

"Mean Gene! Mean Gene! Know nothing about Mean Gene!"

My hunch was that I had to be very gentle with Lyle. The nightmare of a train wrecking his body, and the secret he had lived with for so many years, may have damaged his mind beyond repair.

"Mean Gene won't be able to hurt you, Lyle. Not here in the street mission."

Lyle shook his head again.

"Many people are in danger, Lyle. My brother. My friends. Maybe others. You must tell me."

He shook his head harder. His beard brushed side to side against his arms.

What was the key to making him reveal his secret? Whatever it was that kept him afraid.

Suddenly I knew what to say.

"Lyle. We know about the subway. Now that we know, too, Mean Gene can't hurt you. And you won't be sent to jail for something that happened so long ago."

He wanted to believe me.

It was Lisa who broke the barrier. She had been sitting

quietly, even though the conversation made little sense to her. She placed her hands on Lyle's and nodded at him. The tiny man came to a decision, and it seemed to break a dam within him.

"Safe here? No Mean Gene? No jail for Lyle?"

I sighed deeply. It had worked. "No, Lyle. Jail for Mean Gene. And you will be a hero."

"A hero." Lyle sighed in satisfaction, then his eyes flickered at his memories. "Took me from a corner, Mean Gene did. Rolled me to the top of a hill and pointed me down. So steep, the hill!"

The tiny man shivered. "Said he would let go! Make me into a race car down the sidewalk! So I told him of the secret place below the streets."

Lyle's eyes became wild, and he cackled lightly. "He wanted the money! The money! All for himself."

"One hundred thousand dollars," I said.

"Yes! Yes! My money! But for years I had no legs to get it! Nobody to trust!"

Lisa followed our conversation in silence, her head turning from Lyle to me to Lyle like watching a tennis ball over the net.

Lyle's face darkened. "Then he said if I told anyone else, he would send the police to put me in jail. Wheelchair enough jail for Lyle!"

It made sense. Once Mean Gene knew about the hideout, and the money, he needed a way to keep Lyle silent. Blackmail.

But something puzzled me. "If you could tell no one else, why make that offer to Mike and me when we first saw you? Why put the paper in my pocket this afternoon?"

He cackled again. The poor man slipped in and out of his craziness even as he spoke to us. "Have you ever put your foot into a cold lake? Have you ever stood on the edge of a high diving board and looked down?"

I understood. Wanting to do something and becoming afraid at the last possible moment.

Lisa could stand it no more. "Will one of you two explain what is going on here?"

I guess I wanted to show off. It was, after all, Lisa.

"Lyle robbed a bank," I said. "He robbed it in 1959. He had an almost foolproof getaway plan. A secret hideaway somewhere in the subway tunnels."

I gave Lisa the newspaper clipping. It described the bank robber being chased on foot by policemen to a subway entrance at Broadway and West Fifty-fifth, which was the phrase that had caught my eye at the diner as Hugo was speaking. The police immediately had all subway trains stopped and sealed. To them, it was only a matter of going through all the trains.

"But," I said, "the police were wrong. They assumed a robber runs into a subway station to catch a getaway train. They didn't know this robber was going to run down the tracks and never get on a train."

"So they never found him," Lisa said. "Which is exactly what this old newspaper article describes."

"Yes. Remember the guy in the warehouse? He told us Mean Gene Delaney vanished along the tracks. The same type of disappearance, years and years later. It was too much of a coincidence."

I turned to the tiny man in the wheelchair.

"This is my guess, Lyle. You hid the money and waited until it was safe to leave the tunnel that night. Maybe a month or two after the robbery, when the police had given up, you returned to get your money. Except on the way in—because if it was on the way out you would have been found with the money—you misjudged something, and a train hit you. And once you were in a wheelchair, there was no way to get the money without help. Who could you trust?"

Later, because you can't describe a man as crazy right in front of him, I told Lisa that as Lyle started losing his mind, he would have babbled about the money much as he did in front of Mike and me. And that Mean Gene Delaney must have made the connection between the bank robbery and his subway accident, much as I did.

I leaned forward. This was the most important part, the part I could not know without Lyle's help.

"Lyle, please tell us what you told Mean Gene Delaney. Tell us where the secret hideaway is."

The tiny man's eyes became dreamy. "Hideaway. My father's mistake. He was an engineer."

I nodded, a little impatient. I wanted to get to Joel. And to Mike and Ralphy if Mean Gene had spotted them at Broadway and West Fifty-fifth. After all, the man in the trench coat with the hat would certainly recognize Mike.

Lyle kept speaking, sometimes sounding very intelligent, sometimes sounding crazy. "Head engineer! Head engineer!"

The next twenty minutes were painfully slow. Lyle insisted on cackling and wheezing his way through his entire story as we sat, anxious to begin finding Joel. But Lyle would not rest until we understood everything.

As best as I could understand, when he was a very young man, Lyle's father was head engineer of the original subway project in the early 1900s. At Broadway and West Fifty-fifth, he made a tiny error that nearly cost him his job and his reputation. Where the track veered on his blueprint, one letter was smeared slightly. The curve needed to veer five degrees west. The *W* for west looked almost like an *E* for east. To an engineer totally familiar with the plan, there was no need to make it clear that the track had to veer west. It was silly to think otherwise, so he didn't bother mentioning it.

Lyle's father got sick and needed to take four days off work. When he returned, he found to his horror that the foreman and the workers had made four days of progress in the wrong direction. They had misread the blueprints, and the tunnel was extended five degrees east instead of five degrees west.

To save his career, he quickly ordered the work crew to begin again where the track properly needed to curve west. They were told the short four-day tunnel was part of the venting system to keep the tunnel air breathable for passengers. Lyle's father designed a special vent entrance to hide his mistake and keep the crew from suspecting anything different. Then he doctored all the work reports, and nobody else ever knew about it.

The engineer kept that secret until just before he died. He unburdened himself on his son, Lyle, to clear his conscience. Things went bad in Lyle's life, and he became desperate enough to plan a bank robbery, keeping in mind the perfect escape down the subway.

Recalling that part drove Lyle into a hysterical cackle. "And the train nearly killed me! That was my punishment. I went in for the money and the train came before I could reach the vent!"

"Lyle," I pleaded. "Where is the entrance?"

He looked at me with puzzled eyes. "Where the curve begins to turn west. Didn't you listen? The east tunnel, the mistake, is across the tunnel. Turn sideways to slip inside. Little time, little room to make it before the train!"

The answer we needed. Finally. We had to get moving.

"Thank you, Lyle." I shook his hand. "Thank you very much!"

I stood and Lisa stood with me. Just before I turned to begin running, Lisa placed her hand on my arm.

"Shouldn't you leave a note for Brother Phillip?"

I smacked my head. "Of course!"

"And don't you want to ask about the money? Returning it may clear Lyle!"

I grinned sheepishly. "That too."

I turned to Lyle to ask, but it was too late. Lisa's blurted statement had sent him into spiels of cackling. We watched with sorrow for the broken man.

He finally stopped and wiped his mouth to clear the drool falling into his beard.

"Money? Money? That's the worst part of it all! I couldn't tell Mean Gene Delaney even if I wanted!"

"What!" I said.

"Yes! Yes!" Intelligence had left his eyes again. "Don't you understand? I can't remember!" He burst into more hideous cackling. "I can't remember!"

CHAPTER 23

My legs ached, I wanted to be running so badly. *I know where Joel is!*

My hand couldn't write fast enough as I scrawled a note for Brother Phillip. I folded it and gave it to Duke.

"If Brother Phillip comes back before we do, will you please give him this?"

Duke said, "But he—" then stopped and nodded. Twice in one night, breaking off halfway through a sentence. I should have suspected something. But I was in a hurry.

In fact, I wanted to thank him for risking himself to help us find Joel, but time was pressing too hard. As soon as he took the note from my hand, I whirled to run for the door where Lisa was waiting.

We dashed down the sidewalk, not stopping once the entire eight blocks to Broadway and West Fifty-fifth. We didn't speak until we were on the escalators going down.

Lisa gasped, "What next?"

"We'll . . . we'll—" I stopped. I hadn't thought this far. I hadn't considered any danger, either, but seeing the platform loom closer reminded me that it would be no easy task to walk through the tunnel.

"We'll find Mike and Ralphy," I said as we neared the bottom. "Then one of us will have to go through the tunnel and make it inside the vent. If Joel's there, we'll call the police."

The platform was still busy with people. We didn't want to draw attention to ourselves, so our search was careful and slow. Five minutes later the worst of our fears seemed true. Mike and Ralphy were missing, too!

"I don't want to do this," I said. "But someone needs to go into the tunnel, and it's not going to be you."

Lisa's eyes blazed. "Because I'm a girl? I can do it, too."

"No. Because it's my brother."

That brought home the seriousness of our situation. We were quiet as we moved past people to the far end of the platform.

I had wondered how Mean Gene could get on and off the tracks as often as he did without being seen. I found my answer. It was a huge pillar that cast a black shadow on the final section of platform before the tunnel began.

Lisa and I moved into the darkness.

"Spooky," she whispered.

"At least there's a ladder down to the tracks," I said. "Probably for workmen."

A huge headlight grew stronger from inside the tunnel. Immediately we could feel the wind as the train pushed air ahead of it at high speed. We stepped back and thirty seconds later, *whooooosh*, the train whizzed past, stopping quickly farther down the platform.

Lisa was shaking.

"It'll be okay," I said.

"No. It's not that. Look!"

Stuck to a rough edge of the steel ladder was a brightly colored piece of cloth. I recognized it immediately. Mike's shirt. Part of his shirt had ripped! Somebody had taken him this way!

I knew if I thought about it, I would lose my courage.

"Lisa, I timed the trains while I was begging this morning. We've got two minutes until the next one arrives! Wait here. If I'm not back in twenty minutes, get help."

I jumped down before she could protest and before I could change my mind.

The tunnel smelled of old oil. Dim lights, protected by metal baskets, barely glowed every two hundred feet. Water dripped onto my head as I hurried along the tracks. *How much time is left? Where does the track veer?*

As I ran, I could feel the faint rumblings of faraway trains. This was not my idea of fun in Manhattan.

Finally, ahead, I saw where the dim lights began to turn. The curve of the track! All I needed to find was—

Wind started pushing my face! *A train!* The tracks began to shake. I broke into a sprint, still unsure of where to find the vent. The wind began to feel like a hurricane, and still nothing on the side of the tunnel showed me a place to escape.

Could I turn and run back? Was there enough time?

The answer suddenly gleamed against one side of the tunnel. A train headlight bouncing off the wall! I had no choice but to find the vent ahead of me!

The hurricane became a roar and the gleam became a steady light. It was enough light to see! Surely the vent was—

I saw it! Ahead and to the right, just as Lyle had promised. In the light from the train, I saw a dark shadow a foot wide, as high as a tall man, with just enough room to slip in sideways.

The headlight bore down on me, blinding me, and still I ran, rubbing hard against the wall, waiting to fall through the gap in the vent.

When it seemed that there was nothing left, no hope, no more air in my lungs, no more distance between me and the roaring monster bearing down, I fell. I fell through the tunnel wall into safety and the roar continued past me.

I was in complete darkness.

I sat there for minutes, just breathing, still scared about continuing ahead. Was Mean Gene Delaney waiting?

When strength returned to my legs, I felt around. Behind me, the subway tracks. At both sides of me, cool metal. Ahead, darkness and empty space.

The entrance was U-shaped. You took one step straight ahead into the vent entrance, turned left and moved two steps, turned right and moved one more step, then turned right again. I learned all of this the hard way—with the end of my nose and some bruised knuckles.

If Mean Gene Delaney had been there, he would have nabbed me in no time. Which is how much warning I had before falling again—face first into the hideaway.

From the ground, all I saw were feet.

I pushed myself up and looked straight into the eyes of the dusky-skinned dark-haired girl who had pleaded earlier in the day for me to stay near the warehouse.

She said nothing.

She couldn't.

Her mouth was taped firmly shut.

CHAPTER 24

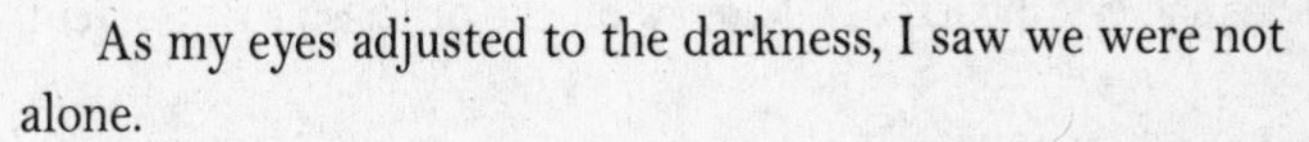

As my eyes adjusted to the darkness, I saw we were not alone.

She was on a battered wooden chair in front of me.

Beyond her, light from gas lanterns showed that the tunnel was as wide as a train, walls and floors of packed dirt. The tunnel extended away from me the distance from first to second base and ended where a canvas flap hung down as a wall. Support beams crisscrossed in all directions. A water pipe at floor level ran the length of the tunnel, wide enough to provide a seat, something quite obvious to me because the pipe was already holding a full audience.

They didn't applaud at my stumbling entrance. Each of them was securely taped—hands together behind their backs, feet together, and, like the dusky-skinned girl, their mouths covered with another strip of wide tape.

By their black T-shirts and ponytails, I recognized them as members of the street gang.

The shock wore off quickly. Taped, they couldn't harm me, and I cared far more about my brother.

I felt panic, I was so frantic to find Joel now that he was nearby.

Just before shouting is when you take a quick deep breath to fill your lungs with air. I'm glad the dusky-skinned girl was smart enough to know that.

I sucked in more than enough air to bellow across the city for my brother, and her eyes widened in horror.

"Mmmmppphhhh!" She shook her head madly. "Mmmmppphhhh!"

It stopped me before I could start.

"Huh?" I said quietly.

She nodded frantically at the canvas wall. "Mmmpphhh!"

I placed my hand against her forehead and tugged at the tape across her mouth, ready to slap it back on tight if she tried anything strange.

It took three tugs before finally releasing with a sticky rip.

She panted for air.

"Quiet!" she said hoarsely. "They're on the other side of the tent wall!"

"The gang?"

She spat with scorn. "Eight of them. All terrible men." It came out as *terreeeeble.* A Spanish accent? She whispered again. "Weeth them, your friends. And your brother." She took another breath. "And my brother."

Her brother?

She said urgently, "They are planning what to do with us. Our only chance is your help now. Then we help you."

"We?" I pointed at the street gang.

"Older brothers and friends from the *barrios.* We have been looking for weeks for this."

Dare I trust her?

Her brown eyes filled with tears as she watched the struggle on my face.

I looked around once more. Sometimes you have a moment of absolute clearness. Everything stops and your mind is focused as sharply as the edge of a razor. It happened then for me.

I decided she was telling the truth. Deep inside me I knew it, just as I suddenly knew there was only one way of winning and that I had to act on it without slowing down to doubt my actions. Maybe I should have turned and run out again to get the police. But Joel filled my mind. I wanted him back, now, and I didn't dare leave.

I left the girl taped to the chair.

"Reeecky!" she pleaded with a whisper.

I ignored her and scuttled to a coil of wire I had spotted lying against a support beam.

I wrapped one end around the beam in front of the tunnel wall nearest the canvas.

"Kid." I jumped. Then relaxed slightly. It was a low growl on the other side of the tent, directed at someone else. "Tell us why you were hanging around the subway station, or it'll go bad on your little friend here."

There was a tiny yelp. *Joel!* My blood raged, and it was all I could do to keep from throwing myself through the flap entrance of the canvas wall.

I didn't wait to hear the reply. The wire was secure around the beam, and I quickly moved to the first member of the street gang on the pipe.

There was enough room between the pipe and the wall for me to move behind the pipe and start tugging at the tape on his hands.

"When you're free," I whispered in his ear, "leave the tape on your mouth. Keep your hands behind your back and your feet underneath you. Got that? Don't move! If they come back before all of you are untaped, I don't want them knowing some of you are free."

As I pulled at the tape, he shook his head downward and to the side. I understood immediately. The handle of a switchblade was sticking out of his pants!

In Jamesville, we usually carry pocketknives for whittling, not for social status. I had no idea how to get the blade out of a switchblade, and when I pushed a button, it popped, slashing three of my fingers.

Later, I told myself. *Fingers heal later, but brothers aren't replaced too easily.*

The blade was deadly sharp and sliced between his hands through the tape. I did the same immediately to his feet. "Remember, don't move!"

He stayed completely still. I repeated my instructions as I went down the line.

Ten free, four to go!

I heard another tiny yelp.

Then Mike's voice, yelling. "I can't tell you more! Now leave him alone!"

Two to go.

Then I froze where I was crouched behind the pipe.

A man had walked through the vented canvas opening.

CHAPTER 25

The man was tall, with cropped gray-blond hair and a hooked nose. I shivered to see the evil in his face as he surveyed the members of the street gang lined along the pipe.

Would one of them lose his nerve and break like a rabbit from the grass?

I held my breath. No one flinched.

"Punks," the man muttered, then strode to the canvas wall and let himself through the flap.

His voice carried back to us as he spoke to the unseen men on the other side of the canvas. "Get ready to move. Now! It's time for us to split."

"What about all these kids?" The question was muffled.

"Leave them taped. They stay. If someone finds them, fine. We'll be long gone. If someone doesn't, too bad. It's not our fault if they starve." A pause, then his voice said roughly, "You two. Come with me."

He was returning! The time to move was now!

I placed the switchblade in the hands of the person I had just released. "Finish up!" I whispered, motioning all of them to stay in place.

Then I raced back toward the canvas.

I found the end of the wire I had left on the ground and wrapped it around a small stick. I sat behind the pipe and braced my back against the wall while pushing hard at the pipe with both my feet. I gripped both ends of the stick and waited.

From the center of my stick, the wire trailed back to the beam, like the rope leaving the handle from a water skier. I kept it slack.

I can't explain how I had thought of the plan. In that moment of intense concentration, I had seen the wire, had seen the beam near the canvas, and the only solution possible had jumped into my head. *Free the street gang! Use the wire to foil Mean Gene!*

Because of it, my body was on automatic, working quickly and without panic, despite my frantic fear. Good thing—there was no time to think.

The two guys closest to me on the pipe stared in puzzlement.

"Grab some tape," I whispered. Rolls of it lay scattered across the floor. Obviously Mean Gene was used to keeping captives. "You'll have your chance soon."

The flap of the canvas shook and Mean Gene walked through, hurrying back to the subway vent.

As he reached the spot where my wire was lying slack on the ground, I pulled hard and tight. *Twang!*

It caught him just above the ankles. He tumbled forward, too surprised to even cough. Almost before he landed, three guys from the pipe pounced on his back. They whipped the tape around his head to cover his mouth, then around his hands and feet, and dragged him behind the large pipe.

It worked!

But how many were left on the other side? Was there a guarantee they would come out one by one? I didn't think so.

I had to get them running out all at once.

Inspiration again!

"Get ready!" I hissed to everyone along the pipe.

I shouted. I shouted good and I shouted loud.

"The money! The bank money! Come back here with the bank money!"

Seconds later, like rats fleeing a burning box, they poured through the flap of the canvas wall.

Three, two, one, and . . . yank!

The wire across the tunnel held straight and true, and the charging bodies from the canvas fell like bowling pins. With screeching howls, the street gang members left the water pipe.

The fight was short and unfair. Fourteen hard and tough and very angry street gang kids stormed against eight dazed and bewildered beggars heaped on the ground.

I didn't wait to see it finish. Joel was there, across the canvas wall! Was he still okay?

Nothing could have prepared me for the sight when I pulled back the flap. I counted a half dozen boys and girls no bigger than Joel, all looking mournfully at me from mats strewn across the floor. Mike was tied to a chair; Ralphy was tied and sitting on the ground behind him. And Joel was on the mat closest to Mike, smiling at me, despite angry red marks where they had been pressing a knife point against his arm to make Mike talk.

It would be a while, a long while, before I forgot the way my heart clutched at my ribs to see Joel's face.

"It's over, Joel," I said. "You're safe now."

He stood up and yawned. "That's good."

Yawning? Like, was this a picnic? The thing that had kept me going in desperation was the thought of Joel spending every second in terror, his tear-filled eyes searching each face among the crowds for mine. And here he was yawning and stretching like it was the end of a nap?

"Don't you get it, Joel? You're safe. No more bad guys."

It didn't interrupt his luxurious stretch for a second.

I tried once more for a bit of gratitude. Stupid kid.

"Hey! You were kidnapped by evil men in the middle of New York City. Weren't you worried? Even for a minute?" I glared at him.

"Not scared." He shrugged. "Knew you would come get me."

Who would think that such total trust could make a person cry?

Mike was smart enough to say he never noticed, even though suspicious-looking drops spattered the dust at his feet while I was untying him. And Ralphy never did ask for his handkerchief back.

CHAPTER 26

Most of it was cleaned up by the time Mike and Ralphy and I led the remaining children back through the canvas.

The dusky-skinned girl saw us and yelped with pleasure. She ran forward and scooped one of the children into her arms.

"Pascale!" she sighed. "We missed you! Oh, we missed you!"

At least *her* brother looked surprised and happy.

Then she set him down.

The beggars were taped securely and propped against the wall. The fourteen street gang fighters guarded them, smiling to watch the dusky-skinned girl with her brother.

"Reeecky, thank you so much," she said. "I, Imalda Vasquez, thank you on behalf of my entire family."

She was nearly as tall as I was. Which was confirmed when she gave me a hug and kissed my cheek. This kissing business was addictive.

"Oh, we do this sort of thing all the time," I replied when she let go. People *have* to act cool around good-looking girls. It's part of the rules, isn't it?

Imalda giggled. "Sure. That's why you and your friend hold hands with a teddy bear in the middle of Central Park."

Ooops. I'd forgotten it was her behind the bush.

Then I remembered I was confused.

"How come all of you were in here when I got in?"

"I was caught spying on your two friends. When my brothers tried to rescue me, the evil one there"—she pointed at the man with the hooked nose and the purple, angry face—"put a knife at my throat and told them to follow quietly or else. When we reached the dark part of the platform, he counted all of us. He told them if even one was gone when he returned, my blood would be on their hands. Then he brought me in first, and between train runs brought the rest in. What could they do but obey?"

It made sense. Terrible sense.

"You weren't after us at all, were you?"

"No. I heard you talk about a missing brother in the diner. I thought if you found yours, I might find mine. I was right." Imalda smiled.

"Why didn't you tell us? It could have saved a lot of confusion."

"I tried. But you kept running away. First in the park. Then at the warehouse."

I snorted. "The people you hang around with don't exactly encourage small talk."

Joel was scratching at the ground near a beam. He'd drive me crazy. "Joel, you know Mom doesn't like it when you play in the dirt." As if his hands weren't filthy enough by now.

"People?" Imalda laughed. "You mean my brothers and their friends."

"Not to insult them," I said quickly. I looked over, thankful that the tough-looking gang was on my side. They grinned at me.

I continued. "Yeah. And the guy in the—"

It hit me. *The guy in the trench coat!* I pointed at the man with close-cropped gray-blond hair and a hooked nose. "Isn't that Mean Gene Delaney?"

Imalda nodded, a puzzled frown on her face.

"Why were you spending time with him?" I asked.

"I wasn't," she said. "How could you possibly think that?"

"But in the park, he chased us as soon as we caught you behind the bush. At the warehouse, he was inside the doorway as you chased us to the fence. I don't get it."

The problem was irritating me, and Joel gave me a place to let off steam. "Joel," I snapped, "can you stay out of the dirt for just a minute? We're not at home, you know."

Imalda frowned harder, then her face brightened. "Oh. Him! That wasn't Mean Gene Delaney. That was—"

She stopped. "I can't tell you," she said. "It was my promise in exchange for help."

"This is crazy. What help?" I remembered something else. "And how did you know my name?"

"I can't tell you that, either."

"Joel!" I nearly shouted, I was so angry at all the confusion. "If you don't leave that dirt alone, I'll strangle your teddy bear." To think, only an hour ago I was ready to give him my entire comic book collection, just to be able to see his face.

Before I could say anything else, there was a banging against the vent entrance. Someone walked through!

All I could see was a trench coat and hat. The shadows covered his face. But nobody moved at the new threat, not even one of the street gang members!

Do Mike and Ralphy and I have to do it all?

"Mike, Ralphy! Now!"

They read my mind. Nobody was going to beat us this late in the game. We rushed forward and tackled.

The man was too surprised to react, and our quick attack worked. He was on his back before he could take a step.

I was on his stomach and Ralphy on his legs and Mike was lying across his face.

"Mmmmmppphhhh! Mmmmmmppppphhhhh!"

"Imalda! Do something! Quick! Hand me some tape!"

She giggled. "I think you should let him go."

"Huh?"

She nodded. Mike slowly got up. Ralphy and I stood back.

The man lifted his crushed hat off his face and gave a painful half smile.

Brother Phillip?

A shout came from behind me. "Hey! Look at what the kid found!"

I didn't turn to look. I was too dazed. *Brother Phillip?*

To add to the confusion, three policemen—one at a time—stepped through the vent entrance.

Brother Phillip?

Joel placed a wad of hundred dollar bills in my hand.

CHAPTER 27

There is no way I can explain it.

Sure, I can explain Brother Phillip. I can even explain Mean Gene Delaney. But there is no way I can explain Joel.

Brother Phillip? When I told him that night in the diner there was no way he could send us back to the safety of the hotel, he made a quick decision. He decided to let us wander the streets under the illusion we were alone. He quickly borrowed Hugo's trench coat and hat and followed us, ready to step in if it looked as if we were in danger.

When Mike and I caught Imalda behind the bushes, what we didn't know was that her brothers and friends were approaching us from the other side. Brother Phillip saw them and thought we were in extreme danger, so he ran from *his* hiding place to help. Embarrassing, or what? Our being followed from three sides and not having a clue.

Then, because Imalda and the street gang disappeared as soon as we ran, Brother Phillip didn't have a chance to find out why *they* were following us. So he thought of a way to catch our followers in a place where he had room to maneuver—he sent us to the warehouse with its wide-open parking lot.

It worked for him. He caught up to them while we were inside and found out they, too, were searching for a lost brother. Brother Phillip, of course, still wanted it secret that he was guarding us. He made them promise not to tell, but he stepped out of the warehouse door too early as they ran to the fence, where once again I spotted him.

That night, naturally, Duke didn't have a chance to give my note to Brother Phillip. Brother Phillip was on the streets looking for us. Hugo had frantically called after we dashed out of the diner, and Brother Phillip had left the mission to try finding us. When Brother Phillip couldn't locate us, he returned to the mission, got the message, and made it to the subway tracks, where he found Lisa on the platform. Then he led the policemen to the abandoned tunnel and stepped through to be tackled by Mike, Ralphy, and me.

Mean Gene Delaney? He'd been around the streets enough to know that Lyle babbled crazily about a bank robbery. When he heard how Lyle had been crippled, he decided it was worth spending some time in research, and he found the newspaper stories in the archives at the library. From there, it was easy to get the information from Lyle. When he couldn't find the bank money, he decided to take advantage of the hideout. Over the months, he slowly recruited other street people to beg, and they kidnapped children to use as props.

But Joel finding the bank money? There is no way to explain that. I doubt Joel was even looking for it. All he wanted was his teddy bear.

The nearest I can explain is that it is part of Joel's radar. He sneaks up on people like a ghost. He tames wild animals like a saint. And he sits beside an old wood beam because he is tired, and finds a tiny piece of burlap sticking out of the dirt. Because he has nothing to do but wait to be taken back to his teddy bear, when the corner of burlap won't pull free, he begins digging.

And finds a hundred thousand dollars. He'll drive me crazy.

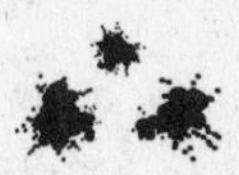

The tracks were silent. All of us—Joel, Imalda holding Pascale's hand, the other kids, Mean Gene, the street gang, the policemen escorting the beggars who stumbled along with their hands taped, Mike carrying a sackful of money, Brother Phillip, Ralphy, and me—formed a line back to the platform.

We climbed up the ladder, and when we stepped around the pillar, it was like fireworks. It was a tossing sea of flashing cameras and bright, bright television lights as journalists fought for position.

In the dazzling glare, I could see a rope holding all of them back.

"What happened in there?"—"How much money?"—"Anybody hurt?"—"What are their names?"

The police left us to talk to the reporters.

Lisa stepped forward from two other policemen. "Sorry, Ricky. I had to call for help, you were gone so long. When the police finally believed me, they shut the trains down. That got all the newspaper and television people here."

She suddenly gasped. "Your hand! What did you do?"

In the excitement, I had forgotten about the switchblade. My fingers were still bleeding bright red drops.

"Ah, it's nothing," I said, remembering my rule about acting cool in front of pretty girls. Although now that she had reminded me of the cuts, they hurt like crazy.

Imalda broke forward. "Reeecky! Let me help." She pulled a scarf from her pocket and grabbed my hand.

That's the photograph most of the papers used on their front pages. Lisa glaring at Imalda. Imalda glaring back. Me on the ground between them where I had fallen after they pulled from both sides. And, dimly in the background, the last part of Joel's leg as he melted away to spy from a safe place.

Epilogue

Our airplane began its descent. I knew that because every flight attendant on board had stopped by twice to see if Joel was okay and to give him and his teddy bear one last cuddle.

Oh well. Life was normal again.

We broke through a layer of clouds and I could see the patchwork of fields far below. Quite a difference from the skyscrapers we had left a few hours earlier.

Mike, Ralphy, and I were flat broke. That's what happens when you have to run around a big hotel and buy every newspaper in sight just so Mr. Evans and Mrs. Thompson and Mrs. Bradley won't spot your photograph on the front page.

On the way to the hotel, Mike had convinced the police to simply bring Joel to Mr. Evans without mentioning our own actions in the rescue. Mike had said all of us were shy about attention and were just happy to have Joel back. Which was all true. We had good reason to be shy about the limelight. But then every morning edition screamed out the bank-money recovery and the breaking of a kidnapping ring.

Fortunately, there had been such a rush to get ready to return to Jamesville that Mr. Evans didn't have time to buy a paper anywhere else. Good thing. It would have taken all the reward money from finding the hundred thousand dollars to dash ahead and empty every newsstand along the way.

Not that we had any of *that* money ourselves, though Mike and Ralphy and I had been determined to keep at least some of the reward. Standing on the subway platform after the reporters had finally left, we argued over what to do with it until Lisa mentioned it would be difficult to explain our involvement that night to parents. So she got her way. None went for new computers, skateboards, or comic book collections. All of it went to the mission center.

That's when Brother Phillip had answered the biggest mystery of the trip for me.

"Joel's safe now," I had said. "So I hope I can bother you with something else that needs help. Something I can't seem to answer on my own."

Brother Phillip gazed calmly as I rushed on. I didn't ever want to doubt God's love, and I thought it was the type of question Brother Phillip would have asked himself many times.

"Why does God let so many people suffer?" I asked. "These beggars and street people hurt so much, and God could take away all their pain so easily."

Brother Phillip's look was wise and sad. "I'm glad you know God has that power, Ricky. And that's why it's such a difficult question. Great men have spent their entire lives trying to answer it."

Then he put his hand on my shoulder. "The best I can tell you is this. It isn't God who makes it bad. It's us. When people choose evil, it spreads like ripples from a stone dropped in the middle of a pool and affects all of us."

He must have read the doubt on my face. He continued. "Some of the street people decide to give up, to take the easy way. It's their choice of lifestyle that brings them suffering. You can't blame God for that."

I protested. "Some of them can't help themselves. What about them? The ones that are sick in the—"

He smiled to interrupt me. "You're right. Others are mentally troubled—it's not their fault that they can't cope. That is where our freedom of choice comes in. We can decide to help them."

He watched me carefully to see if I understood and then said, "Unfortunately, pain and suffering happen as a result of the bad choices we make. But God takes that pain and suffering and uses it in the best possible way."

"Best way?"

"Yes. With pain, we have the chance to be heroes." He grinned. "Heroes in the real sense, not the newspaper sense. Mothers sacrificing for children, friends sacrificing for friends, strangers sacrificing for strangers. Helping those who can't help themselves. Good, too, can be spread like ripples. Except *those* ripples become waves."

I remembered that as the airplane landed.

Our secret involvement didn't stay secret too long.

Mom and Dad and my baby sister, Rachel, were at the airport waiting for us, grateful for the reason that their own flight to New York was no longer needed.

We had been in the car no more than two minutes when Joel reached into his jacket and pulled out a newspaper. Naturally, it was one of the newspapers we had been trying to hide.

"Give it here," I hissed. I hoped this might be a time that Rachel would start fussing in her car seat and provide a good distraction. But she slept solidly as I grabbed for the paper.

I was too late. In a split second, Joel had wasted the entire purchasing spree of two hundred newspapers.

Mom turned at the noise of a rattling newspaper and stared right into the front page photograph.

She looked at the photograph and looked at me, then looked at the photograph again.

"Hmmph. You would think a couple of pretty girls like that could find someone more coordinated to fight over."

She turned back to face out the windshield again. Where was the storm I expected?

"Um, pardon me?" I said very quietly.

"Well, let's face it," she said. "Someone who slashes his hand one minute and falls on his back in front of the whole world the next can't be all *that* terrific."

Then she started giggling. Dad joined her and I thought he was going to drive off the road.

"Oh, you poor child," she finally said. "Brother Phillip kept us informed of every move you made."

"Brother Phillip? Where have I heard that name before?"

It didn't work. "Yes," she said. "Brother Phillip. The one you met in the diner. The one who got your names and found out from Hugo where you lived. The one who then called directory assistance and got our phone number."

"Oh. *That* Brother Phillip."

I tried digging my way down out of sight.

"And by the way," Mom said, "it's too late to confess."

Nipped in the bud.

"You think you could wander those streets and not have anyone care? Brother Phillip assured us you were very safe, so both we and Mr. Evans gave him our blessing."

Mr. Evans knew, too? I hoped against hope that I could grow a beard before school started, so he wouldn't recognize me.

"You were very wrong in leaving the hotel to search, Ricky, even though we understand how badly you wanted your brother back."

The one I felt like throwing out the window?

"Ricky, I'm sorry," Dad said. His tone sounded like he was going to tell me that this would hurt him more than me.

"We discussed a solution with Mr. Evans. After all, you deceived him, too." Dad paused. "You and your friends will paint the entire school this summer."

My friends were going to kill me.

Mom's voice softened as she turned around and ran her hand through my hair. "But you were also very brave. It puts us in a dilemma. You also deserve to be rewarded. So this is what we've decided."

I winced. Knowing my parents, it could be anything.

"We've decided to help you paint the school. This way it will be done in less than a week."

Grown-ups. Try figuring them.

"You can explain the switchblade later," she then said calmly. "But take it from Joel, please. It makes me nervous."

I looked across the car seat.

Aaaagh! My honorary gift from the street gang! The one I had hidden so safely in the bottom of my suitcase. The one Joel was now trying to place in one paw of his teddy bear.

It was going to be a long summer.

The Most Fun You Can Have Reading!

Around the World With Christian Heroes!

Travel the globe and go back through time with the TRAILBLAZER BOOKS! Whatever country or time interests you most, chances are there's a TRAILBLAZER BOOK about it. Learn about Christian heroes—their dangerous and exciting lives—through the eyes of a boy or girl about your age.

TRAILBLAZER BOOKS
by Dave and Neta Jackson

Madcap Mysteries With a Message!

Strange things are afoot in the town of Midvale, and Bloodhounds, Inc. is on the case. A detective agency formed by Sean and Melissa Hunter, along with their slobbery bloodhound, Slobs, Bloodhounds, Inc. finds itself on the trail of ghosts, UFOs, and other strange and seemingly supernatural things. With a deep trust in God's protection and some keen investigating, the two teens help bring the bright light of truth into some scary places.

BLOODHOUNDS, INC. by Bill Myers

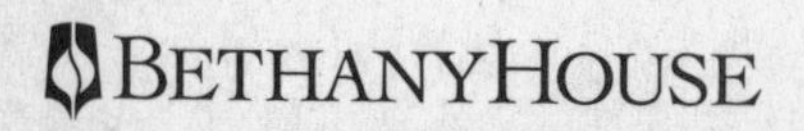